The Mall
The Mannequin Saga

I0672588

Saroj Rathi

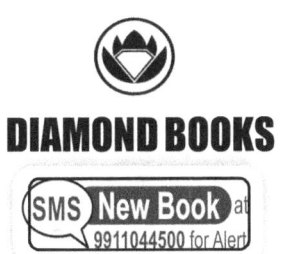

DIAMOND BOOKS

SMS New Book at
9911044500 for Alert

ISBN : 978-81-288-3902-3

© Author

Publisher	: **Diamond Pocket Books (P) Ltd.**
	X-30, Okhla Industrial Area, Phase-II
	New Delhi-110020
Phone	: 011-40712200
E-mail	: sales@dpb.in
Website	: www.diamondbook.in

The Mall
By - *Saroj Rathi*

The Mall

The Mannequin Saga

There is a huge Mall in the city where construction work was still in progress in the midnight hours. All the workers had left but two of them were still there busy with the work. In the dark silence of the night, their excavation work was the only source of noise. Suddenly, one of them stopped.

"I need some rest, I am tired."

"I guess you are well aware of the fact that if we don't finish the work by tomorrow morning, we will be paid partially."

"Dear, why do you always take such jobs at hand that are so strenuous and require more hard work?"

"Because this is more paying. Don't worry; we'll be at complete leisure for the next four days."

A smile appeared on his face as he said "Really!"

"Yes, you have my word."

Both of them again started at a quick pace. After sometime their spade collided with something hard.

"I think something is there."

"Perhaps may be some hidden treasure."

"You are a greedy man. For your general knowledge, I must inform you that before the construction of the Mall there was a hut of a poor magician and not a palace where you can expect to find some hidden treasure."

"How do you know all this?"

"My father told me yesterday. Twenty years ago when this Mall was coming up, he used to work here. The magician was not willing to sell his hut and the garden but his son cheated him and sold it. His hut used to be ancient remains of a palace. The magician was very much attached to it. Once the land was sold nobody saw him again."

"O.K., fine, let's discuss the topic later and have a look what we have found."

Both of them carefully removed the soil and found a skeleton.

"Now what should we do with this?"

"We will inform the Sahib tomorrow about this."

"I fail to understand that when the Mall was constructed why the excavation work was not completed at that time?"

"In those days there used to be a forest here and moreover such big Malls were also not appreciated but now this Mall is surrounded by a full fledged city. The property rates have also hiked up like anything and this requires construction of more shops."

They carefully removed the skeleton and placed it on one side. That very moment the younger of the two noticed something strange.

"See brother, one of its hands is missing."

"It might be somewhere under the ground. We will replace it if we find it. The skeleton will be grateful to us."

Both giggled for a while before starting the work again. After two hours one of them stopped.

"I have finished my work and now I will be heading home."

"Please wait for another ten minutes. I am also about to finish mine and then we will leave together."

Suddenly, they got startled with an abrupt sound.

"Perhaps I have hit something again."

"Let me see, it might be the missing hand."

"You are always kidding."

The younger one quickly removed the soil and pulled the thing out. What he got was a round locket strung in a chain.

"It seems to be of some ancient period."

"See, there is a shinning sun surrounded by four stars on the pendant."

"Now what should we do with this?"

"Let's make the skeleton wear the locket, it will look beautiful."

The younger one did the needful.

"Forgive us, Mr. Skeleton, though we are not able to find your hand but we are returning you your locket."

"Enough dear, now let's get out of here and go home."

Both of them left the place. After a few seconds as the first rays of the Sun fell on the locket, the Sun in the locket started to shine brightly. Gradually the stars also started shining with different colors. The rainbow color emitted by the locket surrounded the skeleton. Eventually the skeleton also started to move and after a while there stood a sixty year old impressive man with long and dense hair, with a bold look on the face and small beard adding more to his attractive personality. He was wearing old fashioned clothes and his shoes were also torn. Perhaps these were the things he was wearing at the time of his death.

He touched the locket and looked around. Then, he noticed his missing hand. He directed the light emitted by the Sun on the locket towards the ground. Soon the bones of his missing hand found its way from beneath the ground and took its destined place. Now, his eyes rested on the monstrous buildings surrounding him.

"I think many years have passed. I have to find out."

He left the Mall; the watchmen were busy and didn't pay any attention towards him. The case was different, he was invisible. He knew it very well that his presence could only be felt by the sense of touch. As he was walking lost in his thoughts, he rushed into one of the security guards coming at a fast pace from the opposite direction. The guard started looking around desperately.

"What happened? You stopped all of a sudden!"

"I just collided with a person."

"And now you are looking for him."

"Yes."

"It's your hallucination. If somebody had been there, I should have also seen. I think you have taken drink again during the working hours."

"No, no."

Then they moved forward quickly.

The invisible man thought, "I must careful with humans."

He saw the terrace of the building and then he closed his eyes. Within a blink he was on the terrace. He stood there viewing the surrounding big elegant buildings, broad roads and running vehicles. The big clock on the Mall told him the time and the year.

Perhaps he was talking to himself, "It has been 20 years since I was dead. God knows where my family is. I just want to meet any member of my family."

He kept sitting there for a long time having locket in his hand and pondering over the past.

His Guru who was suffering from chronicle illness called upon him.

"You asked for me?"

"Yes Saif, I was waiting for you. Come have a seat near me."

The Guru tries to get up but Saif stops him, "Keep lying, you look quite weak."

"I know the time has come. But before I die I want you to have something."

He took out a locket from a small box and gave it to Saif.

"I have taught you all the magic that I knew and this is the last bit of knowledge I possess. This locket has divine powers which are not to be used for selfish motives. I wished my son to inherit it but he is misusing the magic. The power of this locket will guide you to help other people. It can take you anywhere you wish and you can read minds of the people and give life to the lifeless. Once you use it, you will know more about its powers. Make sure, you give it to a responsible and deserving person before you die, otherwise your soul will not rest in peace and if after your death it remains in contact with your body you will get a new life but people will not be able to see or hear you. Only your blood relations will be able hear you."

The Guru was willing to tell something else but his time was over. Saif performed the last rituals. When he reached home his son Monty was waiting for him.

"Where have you been, father?"

"When did you come? You told me that you were suppose to come during the New Year's holiday. How did you manage to take a leave?"

"I have come to take you along. Now you will be staying with us. We will have a bigger house."

"Why? Have you got a jackpot? And is your wife ready to live with me?"

"It is she only who has sent me to take you."

Saif was very happy to hear this from his son. After believing everything that his son said was true, he got ready to go with him. But at that very moment his hand touched the locket lying in his pocket. Now he could read Monty's mind.

'It's been very easy to fool father. He will never come to know that I have sold his land in crores.'

He stood frozen.

"What's the matter father? Why did you stop?"

He didn't feel like telling the truth to his son. He posed as if nothing had happened.

"I want to go after two days as before going, I want to see some of my old friends."

"You know father that I can't stay for so long."

"Alright then, you go, I will join you after two days."

Monty tried his best to convince him. But because of the locket the father was well aware of the wicked plans of the son. In the end, Monty left by saying that he will be back in two days.

Saif spent the whole day in his room thinking about his future plans. He didn't get any sleep in the night. By morning he was ready with a plan. Next day, he went to the market to buy food enough for many days. Then he sealed himself in a secret room in the old house. The room had all the comforts. Monty returned after two days. He could hear Monty's voice. After four days, there was hustle and bustle of people. They were planning to blast away the walls of the old structure. He made up his mind to sacrifice his life. Two more days went by when he heard the blasts. He held the locket tightly and waited for his death. He saw the ceiling fan falling upon him and in an effort to avoid the blow his hand was cut and locket got free.

He tried to get hold of it but as a result of a severe blast the roof engulfed him.

The thoughts of Saif, once again returned to the present. What to do or where to go? He stood confused. The market was already open and people started pouring in. Thinking of getting something he also went inside the Mall. He watched the things on display very carefully. This time he was careful not to collide with anyone. He saw a shining pair of shoes and compared them with his torn off shoes. Out of curiosity he closed his eyes to get a response from the locket, whether he can change his shoes or not? He got the answer. Saif selected a shoe for himself and then placed his old shoe on top of it. Immediately, his shoe was a replica of what he had chosen. He repeated the same process with the second shoe and got the same result. The selected shoes were still there on the rack. He applied the same technique for his clothes as well. Now, he looked like a filthy rich person.

His eyes caught a mannequin in the Mall wearing a beautiful locket. He stood near it.

"Your locket is beautiful, but I cannot change it with mine."

The mannequin answered, "Yours is equally beautiful."

"Thanks." As he spoke he was shocked.

"How strange is that you think."

"More strange is that you can hear me."

"I can listen to the waves emitted from the brain."

"Nobody has been able to hear us so far."

"You are right. I am a dead person."

"So this was the reason that you were avoiding the people walking in the Mall."

"You noticed it!"

"Yes, but I was unable to understand."

"I have lot of things to tell you but the place is getting more and more crowded."

"Yes, you are right. We will talk in the night."

"But where should I go for now?"

"Don't worry. There is a store room in the south-east corner of the Mall. It's a deserted place and you can stay in there."

"Thanks."

"Although, the way to the store room will be very crowded, so please be careful."

"I can go there with the power of my mind."

Within no time he was in the store room. It was quite a huge room having lot of goods stored but still half of the space was empty. Saif selected a place for himself and rested himself over the packed goods. He was eagerly waiting for the night to talk to his new friend.

The officer in-charge responsible for the decoration of the Mall was on a round. He saw the mannequin, the one who was talking with Saif.

He called one of the staff girls, "Mita!"

"Yes Sir."

"Yesterday, I told you to change its clothes and wig as well and also shift it in that corner with a lady mannequin."

In the meantime the girl got busy with her work. On the other hand the mannequin was thinking something else.

"He will not be able to recognize me once my clothes and wig will be changed."

Mita fixed the mannequin as per the instructions and left. The lady mannequin welcomed its new companion.

"It has been quite long since we have met."

There was no answer from the other side.

"What's the matter? Are you not happy to be with me? Last

time when we were separated you looked very upset, but this time I think you want to be with someone else."

"No, the reason is not this, but I am a bit upset."

"Why, what happened?"

"You won't believe me if I tell you."

"Please tell me."

"A few minutes ago, I met a person who could hear us."

"Really! Who was he, what was his name?"

"I forgot to ask this, but he promised to meet me in the night."

"Then, what is the problem?"

"The problem is that these people have changed my looks and clothes, now he will not be able to recognize me."

"Don't worry; if he has the power to listen to us, then he must be capable of recognizing us too."

"I think you are right."

"Now feel free as I have a lot to tell you."

"You and your never ending stories. Sometimes, I am surprised, how can you cook so many stories standing still at a place."

"You are making fun of me. I am not going to tell you anything."

"Oh, please don't take it otherwise, I was just kidding."

As their teasing talks were in progress, the Mall was blossoming with people rushing in and out. On the other hand Saif gathered more and more information from the locket. He was now well aware of the things he can do with it. He decided to stay there only. Gradually, the night creeped in as he was lost in his thoughts. All the lights inside the Mall were switched off. Saif came out of his hiding den, it was pitching dark. He took out his locket, turned the circle at its center and the whole Mall lit on brightly.

Both the mannequins were astonished, "So much light at night?"

"I think it is him only who met me in the morning."

Saif appeared in front of them.

"How are you, my friend?"

"I'm fine. How did you recognize me?"

"Through the powers of my locket."

"See, I told you."

"So you also talk."

"Yes, all the mannequins here can talk but we can not meet each other with our wish as we are unable to move. So to communicate with each other, we use the mind waves. We don't even know from where these powers have come into us?"

"You will know the answers to all your questions soon. Now, tell me your names."

"We don't have names; moreover there is no need of names."

"But without names how shall I address you?"

"Yes, when we have to be together, we must live as friends, whether we like it or not."

"We didn't mean that. In fact, I am a bit frightened by these lights as it will attract lot of attention. The security people must be on their way and you shall be caught."

"You don't worry, nothing will happen. This light is not visible to human beings. It is magical."

"Please tell us about yourself. We are very keen to know about you."

"Sure, first I want all of you to gather at one place."

"You are forgetting the fact that we cannot move on our own so you have to do something. Will you gather us manually?"

"Earlier, you were not able to move but now you can. Just try it."

Both the mannequins tried and they were moving like robots. Though they were not able to show the expression of excitement on their faces, they bowed before Saif to show him gratitude.

"No need of it, now go and assemble all the mannequins near the stairs."

They left. Saif was more than happy as he had lost all his faith in the human beings for which he was not willing to see them. Thinking all this, he reached the stairs and found all the mannequins there. Saif noticed each one of them paying respect to him either by bowing, joining hands or kneeling on the floor. Their presence made the place crowded. Saif made space with his magic and arranged the chairs in a circle. All of them sat on the chairs. Now Saif addressed them —

"I am well aware of your curiosity to know me. My name was Saif and I was a magician. After 20 years of my death, I am alive again just because of the locket gifted by my Guru. Not only me, these dazzling lights and your movement, are all possible through the powers of this locket."

One of the mannequins asked, "You mean to say that all the mannequins are not same as us."

"No, not at all. All of you were near to this locket which was buried somewhere below; its power had a spell on you which I have made more strong. "

A child mannequin spoke, "We are very happy and what should we call you?"

"You can call me Saif, and I will also call you by your names."

The child excitedly said, "But we have no names."

"I will name each one of you."

Saif named the child boy mannequin as John and the girl Jui. Apart from these two, there were four couples of mannequins. The boys were named as August, Sitam, Attu and Amber while the girls were called Jenny, Ferry, Mui and Dish. The first mannequin that Saif came across was named Amber and his friend as Ferry. All were very happy but since their faces were expressionless, neither were they able to move their lips nor they could blink their eye lids so all the talking was done by waving of the hands. All of them were talking except August.

Saif asked, "What's the matter August? Why are you so quiet?"

"Can we talk only during the nights?"

"You can talk to each other any time you want. The rays of the locket will carry your words to each other."

Jui jumped in excitement, "Exactly, like a mobile. Isn't it Saif?"

"Yes, Jui."

"And you will be visiting us during the night only?"

"No, I can also recieve your waves, you can call me anytime."

Sitam asked, "Where will you be during the day?"

"I have not given any thought to it."

Amber, "Don't you like the place I told you?"

"No, the place is good but it is not safe. The goods keep coming and going from place to place. Yesterday also I bumped into a security personnel and I don't want to repeat it."

The darkness outside was now subsiding. Saif told all of them to take their respective places. He re-arranged the furniture as it was earlier. As Saif was leaving Jui called him.

"Have a nice day Saif. We shall meet in the night."

Saif gave a smile to her and left the place. He sat at the top of the Mall planning a city tour. The weather was pleasant and clouds were dominating the sky. There was a strong possibility of heavy rain. Saif knew that rain drops will not affect him. He was enjoying the walking on electric poles and wires. After twenty years it was altogether a new city. Roaming here and there he stopped at a graveyard. The rain had already started by then with strong winds. The people including the watchmen present in the graveyard ran for the shelter. Saif was now walking freely.

"I don't even have a grave. People say, only a small piece of land is needed as one dies, I do not have that too."

He was talking to himself and suddenly his eyes noticed a name-plate on one of the graves. He could not believe his eyes. To make sure he moved closer and he was not wrong. What troubled him was the year mentioned on it.

"It was the same year he had died. It is not possible; there must be another person of the same name."

"He tried to console himself. He looked around; his eyes caught sight of each and every grave nearby. Names on them made him to believe. Drained out of energy, he sat there. These graves were of his son and his daughter-in-law.

"But Manila was pregnant. What happened to her?"

There was nobody to answer his questions. He sat there for a long time. Then, slowly he made his way towards the Mall. He felt like a completely ruined person. Before dying he prayed to God to forgive his son but it seemed that his prayers were in vain.

In the night when all the statues gathered they felt Saif's pain and disappointment. Amber gestured Ferry to ask.

Ferry enquired, "Saif, why are you so upset?"

Saif looked around and told everything about his family. There was pin drop silence for some time.

Then Dish spoke, "This is very sad Saif but you must consider, even if they were alive, they would not be able to see you. Then you would have felt even more helpless."

"This is true, they would not have been able to see me, but they could have heard me and felt me and even I could have done so."

John said, "Don't be sad, we all are your children."

Jui put her hand on Saif to which Saif smiled.

Jui said, "Saif, do you know, today, in the Mall a small kid was pleading her mother to ask me to play with him?"

"What happened then?"

"His mother refused and the child sat on the floor in protest. I enjoyed reading his mind."

"What was going in his mind?"

"He was planning not to listen to his Mother. He was also thinking that on reaching home when she serves him food, he will spill it and he will also not drink the milk."

Jenny said, "Are you talking about the child with curly hairs and red pants?"

"Yes, the same one. Then you must have also read this?"

"When he came closer to me he wanted to get my wrist watch. His mother got him one and he was happy. Then he framed his mother as the best mother in the world."

Saif said, "Children are always like this, in a moment they get angry, and the very next moment they forget everything."

August said, "But as a person grows up, he becomes clever and selfish."

"There are both types of individuals. I also used to be one and I never deceived anyone in my life."

"I didn't mean to say that Saif."

"I know. Now tell me what have you come across in the Mall today?"

"Today two girls visited the Mall and they were best friends. Both wanted to marry the same boy and were here to buy gifts for him. But they were telling lie to each other. The interesting part was both of them were aware of the truth but then they were happy thinking that she is making a fool of her friend."

Attu said, "But there are nice girls too. Mita, the one who works in the Mall is very nice. She always changes my clothes affectionately and also says that she likes me very much."

All eyes turned to Attu. Attu was feeling embarrassed now. "I didn't mean that."

Jenny said, "But we didn't say anything either too."

Everybody laughed and Attu took his leave. This became a daily routine. The mannequins told the day-to-day experiences of the Mall to Saif who in return told them what was happening in the outer world. Some days passed. One particular evening the Mall was very crowded. A beautiful girl was looking curiously at two mannequins. They were Ferry and Amber. Her eyes were glued to the locket in Ferry's neck.

She said to herself, "It is very beautiful but I don't know whether it will suit me or not."

Ferry said, "Sure it will look good on you as you are so beautiful."

"Thanks."

Suddenly the girl got startled.

"I was talking to whom? Who addressed me as beautiful?"

She started looking around her. Everybody was busy shopping and moreover she only thought of it in her mind so how could someone listen to her? She looked at the mannequins but how can they speak? She jerked away the thought as an hallucination and went away."

The moment she left, Ferry said, "She can hear our voice."

"How can this be possible? Whatsoever, we must alert all the mannequins."

Immediately, Ferry transmitted mind waves to all the mannequins, "The girl with pink frock and long hair can listen to us. If she comes across you please remain silent."

The girl passed in front of John and Jui. Sitam also saw her when she was looking at the clothes while standing near Attu. Attu couldn't believe that the girl was capable of hearing them. He decided to test himself.

"You have beautiful hair."

"Thanks."

The girl replied back. But there was nobody. Then she saw Attu, the mannequin.

"What's wrong with me today? Why am I having the feeling, these mannequins are talking to me? If I tell this to anyone he or she will think that I have gone mad. I just hope that I don't loose my future while finding my past."

She left the Mall quickly. At that time Saif was relaxing in his hiding place when he got the mind waves from Amber.

"Where are you Saif, please come immediately."

Saif appeared before Amber within no time. "What's the matter Amber and why have you called me at this crowded hour?"

"Saif! A girl just came in here and she could hear us."

"You must be mistaken."

"No, Saif. You see for yourself. She is wearing a pink frock and her hair is pretty long and beautiful."

Saif quickly searched for her. Attu told him that she had left the Mall. Saif ran outside.

He caught a glimpse of her while she was hiring a taxi. Saif mounted on the roof of the taxi. After some time the taxi crossed the crowded streets in the city and halted in front of an old house. The girl went inside as Saif followed her. Inside the house an old woman was lying on the bed who looked very weak. There were two more women who were taking care of her.

One of them spoke to the girl, "Thank GOD, you have come. Her condition is deteriorating; she was calling for you again and again." They moved closer to her bed.

"Mother! Please open your eyes, your Ice is here."

The weak woman opened her eyes with great effort. She seemed relaxed to see Ice.

In a trembling voice she said, "I never knew that my time will come so early."

"Why are you saying so? You are the only one who knows about my past."

"I am telling you, that only. Did you visit the place I had asked you?"

"Yes, I am coming from there only."

"Did you feel anything?"

"Yes, it seemed like everything over there was trying to talk to me. Initially, I got afraid but I think I will visit the place again."

"You must go there Ice, my child, that place belongs to you. You are the real owner of the land."

"What are you saying?"

The old women gestured towards the girl and handed over a small packet to her. Ice took it looking curiously at the old lady.

"These are the legal papers of that place which are in the name of your grandfather. Your grandfather was a great magician. He never wanted to sell this land but when your father forced he disappeared. Your father repented when he was gone and he changed his mind not to sell the land. The evil people didn't agree to him as he had already made the deal and had taken a handsome amount in advance. They imprisoned your father, Monty and your mother, Manila in their own house. You were only one month old. I was the housekeeper of the house. They live there for two years. They took this house for only two months in order to search for your grandfather. One day when I visited the house I saw two people guarding the house. I had a doubt. I reached the back window of the house. They trusted me and rested you in my hands along with the legal papers. But I was not able to take care of you. One day in my absence my husband sold you to a couple. I hope you will forgive me."

"No, no, you need not ask for forgiveness. They took good care of me. I never felt that I am not their daughter. They provided me with all the comforts which perhaps my parents wouldn't. Last year, my father suffered a major setback in business which he couldn't bear and died. Last month mother also passed away. But before dying she told me the whole story and your address as well. I found it very difficult to find you and now you are also……."

"Don't cry Ice. This packet contains a letter from your father which will tell you all the details. May God help you!"

The old woman closed her eyes. As Ice quietly moved out, Saif followed her. He felt as if his son has just died.

He raised his hands towards the skies and prayed, "Be happy wherever you are."

Ice was walking on the road slowly. Suddenly, she thought of the packet which reminded her of her father's letter. Now she walked briskly towards the hotel where she was staying. Saif followed her. The moment she reached the room she took out all the contents of the packet. There were papers of the land, photographs of her parents and grandfather. Ice stared the photos for quite a long time. Then, she found the envelope containing the letter from her father:

Dear daughter,
I love you. We are the unfortunate parents who were not able to take care of their daughter. Now you are a grown up girl, so you will be able to understand the things. I ditched my father and now I am facing the consequences for the same. I know how it feels when a child is separated from its parents. It is better commit to suicide, then to be murdered by evil hands. But before I die, I want you to know about you grandfather who was a great person. I am quite confident that he is still alive because of the magical locket given to him by his Guru. I got to know this from the Guru's son who himself was desperate to get the locket. You must visit the place where our old house used to be. If you remember him from the core of your heart he will surely meet you.
Your Father,
Monty

Ice placed the letter aside and lied down. Saif read the letter. He was not sure whether he should make Ice aware of his presence or not. He doubted that it might scare Ice. When he looked at Ice she was asleep. He thought it is dark; everyone in the Mall must be waiting. He proceeded towards the Mall.

Seeing him Ferry spoke, "What is it Saif? Did you meet the girl? Who was she? How could she hear us?"

"Oh! So many questions in a row. Will you allow me to take a breath at least?"

"Anyways we don't breathe."

"Oh! I forgot."

Everybody laughed

Then John said, "Come on Saif, now tell us."

"Yes, I am coming to it. She is my granddaughter, the daughter of my son Monty. Since she is my granddaughter, she inherits some of my powers automatically of which she is not aware. I thought I have lost my family but I am fortunate to have her."

"It is surprising that instead of being happy, you look so upset?"

"You are right Jui. I am worried about Ice. She is all alone."

"So, you didn't meet her?"

"No, I thought she might get scared."

"Does she know you?"

"She got to know about me today only and I think she will definitely come to see me tomorrow."

"Surely, she will come, Saif, we all shall help her."

"Thanks a lot."

Now, everyone keenly waited for the next morning. Each of them had a plan. Next day when the Mall opened everyone kept asking Dish as she was placed near the gate. Attu created maximum troubles for her.

"Dish do you think, you will recognize her? It is not necessary that she will be wearing the same pink frock."

Attu kept sending so many messages to which Dish got irritated.

"You know most beautiful mannequin is placed near the gate to attract people."

"That is fine but beauty always doesn't come with brains. Truly speaking, possessing both the thing is a rare combination."

"I don't want to talk to you."

"I also don't want to talk to you. I will talk directly to Saif."

The mannequins were having fun teasing each other, while Saif sat on the roof of the Mall watching carefully all the cars passing by. He didn't have to wait for long. Ice was walking down the road. She was wearing blue denim and white top. She looked pale and tensed. After roaming in the Mall for sometime she reached near Ferry, the mannequin. The moment she saw Ferry something came to her mind. She went closer. Then she said in her mind without speaking, "You spoke to me yesterday, it was not an illusion, and please tell me. Do you know any magician called Saif? I am her granddaughter. I don't know that what my father has written is true or not."

Ferry answered Ice's question, "Whatever your father has written is completely true. All the mannequins of this Mall are friend of your grandfather, because of his powers we are like this."

Ice couldn't believe. She was talking to a mannequin. She was spellbound as she looked at Ferry. As she learnt about her Grandfather, tears rolled down her eyes. Seeing her crying a girl approached her.

"Can I help you Madam? Why are you crying in front of this mannequin?"

Ice composed herself and said, "No, nothing. Something has fallen in my eyes. My eyes are already weak and very sensitive to foreign objects."

Ice managed to take her in confidence and started to look at the displayed items. After a while she again started to talk.

"Where is my grandfather? I want to see him."

"He also wants to meet you Ice. But he is afraid that he might scare you. That's why he is avoiding you."

"Why should I be afraid of my grandfather?"

"It's good to hear that. Now you go to the graveyard, he will meet you there."

"Thanks a lot but what should I call you?"

"I am Ferry and he is my friend Amber."

"It is my pleasure to meet you people."

Amber said, "We feel the same, but yesterday you really scared us."

"How?"

"Because you could hear our conversation."

"Why? Cant the other people listen to you?"

"No, it is not possible. You belong to Saif's family and that is the reason, you can hear us. In fact it is for the first time that we are talking to a living person."

"I am also.......! Hey what should I consider you, dead or alive?"

"We will think of it later, now you must go."

"O.K. I would like to know more about you."

"Your grandfather has answers to all your questions."

Ice left and headed for the graveyard. On her way, she kept thinking of her grandfather who would be quite an old man now. She reached the graveyard; she saw a ray of light. Ice followed it. She was felt as if the light was guiding her somewhere. The rays lead her to the graves of her parents. She was in tears.

"Both of you are here but where is my grandfather?"

Saif who was there said, "I am here my child."

"I can't see you. I want to see you. Is it one of your magic tricks? Please come in front of me."

"This is no magic Ice. You cannot see me."

"Why?"

"Because, I am dead."

Ice started weeping bitterly.

"Calm down my child. I was dead even before you were born but due to this locket I have got a new life."

Saying this Saif patted her head with his hand. Ice experienced a very soothing touch.

"Is this you grandfather, you can touch me."

Yes, we both can touch each other."

Ice took Saif's hand into hers and lied down in his lap. Saif rotated the locket and a bright light entered Ice.

"Grandfather, what was that?"

"I have given you some powers. With the help of these powers you can call me anytime or we can talk to each other through telepathy. Apart from this you can also know what is going in the minds of other people also."

"Grandfather, you can't imagine, how happy I am."

"I know. No one can judge this better than me."

"Grandfather, I want to know about those mannequins."

"Sure, but not here. You go back to your hotel. I will see you there. Here, seeing you talking to the graves, people might think that you have gone crazy."

Ice looked around and noted some eyes staring at her. Getting up she said, "Why don't you come along with me?"

It will be difficult. I might just bang in with someone. You don't worry, I can reach anywhere with my powers."

Ice hired a taxi and headed towards the hotel. She ordered something to eat and closed the door and windows of her room.

Then she murmured, "Grandfather!"

"I am here with you, Ice!"

"Where are you?"

"On the sofa."

Ice also seated herself on the sofa.

"Now you tell me everything about our old house, my father`s childhood, my mother, your magic and the Mall as well. Everything is just like a dream to me."

"O.K. Here I go, first you finish your meal."

"All right, you also have some."

"No, I don't need it."

Saif told Ice each and every detail. Ice listened carefully like a curious child.

"How nice is everything. Will Ferry, Amber, Jui, John, Sitam and rest of the mannequins also be my friends?"

"Sure. Why not?"

"It will be real fun, but how? I cannot go there in the night."

"We will think of something, Now, I should go. It is night already and they will be waiting for me in the Mall. You also go to sleep, I will see you tomorrow."

The very next moment Saif was with the mannequins. All of them stood up at his sight. Saif started narrating himself even before he was asked.

"Ice is my granddaughter. We spoke for a long time. She was not at all afraid of me. She was very happy when I patted her affectionately. The best thing is she wants to be friend with all of you."

"It will be great fun."

"How can it be possible? She cannot visit here at night and if she keeps coming in regularly during the mall timings, she will be suspected."

Jui said, "It is a problem."

Jenny said, "Can't you transfer her with some powers, so she can come here at night?"

"It is quite difficult and will take time too."

August said, "Then, what do you suggest?"

"I am still confused."

Sitam said, "I have an idea."

"Tell us."

"What if Ice joins the Mall? Then she will be able to stay with us for the entire day."

"Great, Sitam. It sounds very nice."

Attu said, "But will she get a job?"

Saif said, "This will not be much of a problem, first I will talk to Ice in the morning."

In the hotel, Ice was trying to sleep. It's been a wonderful day for her. She slept late thinking about the whole day. Next morning, she looked at her watch and it was already past ten. She called her grandfather.

"Where are you grandfather?"

"I am on the roof of the hotel. You get ready then I will come."

"No, you come right now; I want to talk to you."

Saif placed himself on a chair. Ice came to know as the chair moved.

"Grandfather, you should have come into the room instead of sitting on the roof."

"It hardly matters. Today you tell me about yourself."

"My story is very short. The couple who adopted me were very nice. Two years after my adoption, they were blessed with a son but they never made me feel that their love for me has lessened even for a day. Instead they loved me more than before. I learned dance and music. I was good in studies also but before dying my father told my brother that I was not their real child. This changed the attitude of my brother. I helped my father in designing clothes. I had to complete my studies and had to look after my ailing mother so I decided to stay back. As I completed my studies, mother also died, and I left the place in search of my own people."

"Is your brother aware about your being here?"

"No, and will he neither look for me."

"Then you must do something in order to make a living."

"Presently I have some money but it will be gone soon."

"You get some work in the Mall which will also give you a chance to be in the company of the mannequins."

"It's a great idea, but how will these people give me a job?"

"You tell them that you will convince the people to purchase goods which will give a boost their sale."

"Will they believe me?"

"You ask them to keep you on trial basis for a month. I am sure they will definitely agree."

"It's fine. What if I don't live up to their expectations, I am not too sure, as I have no experience in this."

"You don't worry about it. All your new friends will help you in this and moreover I have some magic too."

Ice wanted to say something but Saif stopped her, "No more questions now, get ready and reach the Mall. I will meet you there. One more thing, don't move your lips while talking to me in front of others."

Saif left and Ice dressed herself. She left for the Mall and on reaching the Mall she made a silent prayer.

"O! God, help me today. Get me a job here."

"Everything will be right as Saif is by your side. So you need not worry."

Ice looked at Dish, "How are you, Dish?"

"You know my name?"

"Yes, you all are my friends now so, I have to know your names. You told me something that my grandfather didn't say."

"It is his specialty. He is man of action and not words."

Both of them were talking, a girl came.

"Excuse me Madam, How can I help you? You are staring at this mannequin from a long time. If you like this dress then I am sure it will look nice on you."

"Thanks, but I am not here to purchase, but to find a job. Can you take me to the manager?"

"I don't think it will be of any use. Yesterday only two girls were fired."

"Still I would like to give it a try."

"As you wish, follow me."

Ice followed the girl. On her way all the mannequins wished her good luck. When they entered the manager's office there was a man in his mid forties scribbling through the pages of a file. He looked tense.

He looked at them, "What is it Gunjan?"

"Sir, this girl wants to see you."

"Look, if you are here for a job then I am sorry, I can't help you. The Mall is already suffering from a huge loss."

Ice replied, "If I assure that within a month I can double the sale of the Mall? Then also you are not interested?"

Now the manager started thinking. Ice started reading his mind.

"This girl is making fool of me. How can I get rid of her?"

Ice said spontaneously, "You listen to my plan once. If you don't like it I will leave at once."

"How much time will it take?"

"Only five minutes."

Ice explained him the plan as set by her grandfather and asked him to let her work for a month in order to prove herself. Ice read his mind that he was not willing to pay her for this period.

"Sir, if you do not like my performance, I will not take any salary for one month and will resign."

"Without money you can work as long as you wish."

"One month is sufficient for me."

"You look quite confident. I wish you success. When would you like to join?"

"Tomorrow itself, Sir."

"O.K. fine."

Ice and Gunjan came out.

"You did wonder."

"The real wonder will begin from tomorrow when we start working together. Are you with me?"

"How can I refuse? Anyways there is not much do also in the Mall these days."

"O.K., I will leave as I have to find a house for myself."

"Which house would you prefer?"

"No particular choice for the time being. I have nothing except some clothes."

"I think I can manage a house for you."

Gunjan gave Ice an address and asked her to go there. After promising the mannequins to meet them next day, Ice reached at the address given by Gunjan with his grandfather. A woman opened the door for her.

"Yes?"

"Hello, Aunty. Gunjan has sent me."

"You must be Ice."

"Yes."

"Please, come in."

"Gunjan told me about the vacant flat."

"Yes, be seated. I will get you water."

When both of them were talking Saif had a quick look at the flat. It was quite good with all the basic comforts.

"You have a look at the flat first; we will settle other issues later."

Ice heard her grandfather saying, "I have seen the flat. It is perfectly fine. You can say yes to her."

"It is not required; you just tell me if you have any issue."

Ice started to read her mind quickly. She has liked Ice's innocent face. During the course of conversation the lady told Ice that her son works overseas. She has sufficient money and was only giving the flat on rent because she felt lonely. Soon all the things were settled.

"O.K., Aunty. Now I must go and bring in my stuff. Can I get in a maid to cook food?"

"You can have the food with me."

"But?"

"O.K., you can pay me whatever you like."

"You have solved a big problem for me."

"No, it is you who have solved my problem. You will not understand how difficult it is to cook and eat without any company."

"I can understand Aunty. I have gone through it after my parent's death."

"O.K. then bring in your luggage as soon as possible. Meanwhile I will get your flat cleaned."

While they were leaving Saif said, "Ice you reach hotel, I will pack your luggage."

"Grandfather, I don't like you doing all this."

"Don't worry; I will not do it."

"How will you manage?"

"Now you must understand certain things automatically."

Saif had gone. Ice understood what he meant. Saif reached the hotel room. Sitting on the sofa he started practising his magic. After a long time, it was first time he was not using his locket but performing what his Guru had taught. Everything that belonged to Ice was now moving. A box opened itself and things started to move in. In a few minutes everything was packed. Saif was happy to give his own magical touch.

After sometime they were back at Aunty's place. Ice liked the room very much. Everything needed was available. Ice thought, it must be her son's room, Aunty entered the room.

"This room belongs to my son, I have not allowed anybody to enter this room as I always thought one day he will be back home."

Suddenly, Aunty was sad.

"Don't worry Aunty, I will take good care of the room and his things."

"It is not required. Both of these cupboards are empty. You can arrange your things. Get fresh and come down. Food is ready."

Aunty went downstairs. Ice had a good look at the room. It was a beautiful and elegant room expensively decorated. There was a small hall attached to the room from where the stairs descended. The paintings adorning the walls of the room were highlighting owner's artistic taste. Ice closed the door.

"Grandfather, this is very nice. Exactly like my old house."

"The lady too is very nice. You should take care of her."

"I will try my best to keep her happy."

"I have also got a place for myself. There is a lot of space behind the sofa in the hall. I can rest there and moreover there is no risk of banging in with somebody."

"I am very happy. I never imagined of everything settling so soon. I have nothing to worry when you are with me."

"Ice, my presence is not enough, the goodwill of a person is more important. Today the life is moving at such a pace in which everyone is trying to get ahead of each other. People have forgotten the fact, if they help somebody it will be returned to them two folded."

Both of them kept talking and Ice was arranging her things with Saif's help. Later Ice went downstairs. Aunty was waiting for her.

"It's good, you have come. I was about to come upstairs to call you. I am hungry."

"You must have called me."

"Have you arranged your luggage?"

"Yes, Aunty. Can I know your name?"

"Sunaina."

"What a sweet name!"

"Your Uncle used to say like this."

"He must have looked into your eyes everytime he took your name like this."

"You are a naughty girl!"

Ice's light hearted talk made Aunty happy. Both had their food and kept on talking for a long time. Ice also accompanied her to the market. She wanted to see the market. Both spent a long time in the market. Then Ice forced her for a movie and both enjoyed a lot. After dinner Sunaina thought of the happiness she had after such a long time.

Ice had to go for her job next morning, so she went to bed early. While Sunaina kept staring at her husband's photo on the wall. Lost in the old memories, she fell asleep without medicine which she was taking for many a months.

Next morning everyone had a new energy. Sunaina was fondly preparing breakfast for Ice. Ice was also very excited for her first day on the job. She was happy on the thought of spending the whole day with her new friends. Ice was packing her lunch when Gunjan dropped in. Her house was not very far from there.

"Hi, Gunjan. Come in. Would you like to have breakfast?"

"No, Aunty, I just had."

"Ice, if you are ready then let's go."

"Yes, I am. Tell me how I look?"

"It doesn't make any difference."

"Why?"

"We have to change clothes there."

"Oh! It just slipped my mind."

"I also did the same thing on the first day."

Both laughed. They bid good bye to Aunty and left. Ice heard her grandfather's voice.

"Ice, I am going for some work, you can call me if you need."

"O.K."

"Whom did you say O.K.?"

"No, no Gunjan, I have a habit of talking to myself."

"Then I have to be careful."

"Why?"

"I have heard that such people are affected by evil spirits."

Then she started laughing loudly. Ice saw her from the core of her eyes. In the meantime they reached the Mall. Dish greeted Ice.

"Hello, Ice, you are looking very pretty."

Ice silently replied, "Thanks, Dish. I have to change these clothes."

Gunjan helped Ice with the clothes. Ice looked pretty in the blue dress of the Mall.

Gunjan said, "Oh! Ice, you are looking wonderful in these clothes as well."

"Thanks, now let's go out."

John and Jui were happy to see Ice.

"Dear sister, your good looks will definitely make customers buy."

"I must say, they will forget shopping once they see you."

Ice moved ahead with a smile.

Gunjan introduced her to some girls working in the Mall. Gunjan and other girls went to their respective places. Ice had to look for the customers. She started having a stroll in the Mall. She sent message to all the mannequins.

"You people have to help me, I am bit afraid. If I fail to perform, I will not be able to keep your company."

Amber replied, "You don't have to worry for anything. The day has just begun and people have just started to come. You see what we do."

After sometime Sitam sent her a message, "Ice, there is an old lady in the ladies section who is looking for a dress for her granddaughter. You help her."

Ice reached there within no time and saw an old lady holding many dresses in her hands standing confused."

"Can I help you?"

"How can you? Have you seen my granddaughter?"

"You tell me about her likings, I will understand."

The lady stared at. She thought, she can trust this girl. After talking for sometime Ice took out two frocks but she couldn't decide which one she should select. She closed her eyes.

"What should I do grandfather?"

As her eyes were closed she could see the lady's granddaughter wearing a frock. She opened her eyes and saw that one of the frocks she had selected was the same. Ice suggested the lady to buy the same frock. Ice also suggested her necklace, a pair of shoes and some other items which she had seen. The rich lady was happy to buy those things. Now Ice felt confident. She had no fear now. On her first day Ice helped seven customers with their shopping. The mannequins helped her in every possible way. They searched customers for her and also told her the whereabouts of the items. When she took her leave at night all the employees applauded her.

During the night in her room Ice asked Saif, "Where did you go today, grandfather?"

"I had something important to do."

"What is something which is more important than me?"

Saif smiled, "Ice, I am trying to boost my magical powers, so that we can help more and more people. I go to a lonely place in the forest to practise some chants."

"How long will it take?"

"I can't say exactly."

Seeing Ice thinking, Saif said, "Now you go to sleep since you have to reach Mall tomorrow. I also have to go to Mall now. All of them must be waiting for me."

"You know grandfather, today we had a great time. Everybody helped me. When Dish asked Attu to take off his clothes for a customer, he went mad."

"Were you behind this?"

"No, grandfather, but I could see that Dish was just teasing Attu."

"You are a sensible girl and you have to work hard in the future."

"Yes, grandfather."

"Now go to bed, Goodnight!"

When Saif reached Mall everyone was dancing. He had never seen the mannequins as happy as they were today. John and Jui came to Saif.

"Thanks Saif. It was nice to have Ice here."

Amber said, "Today for the first time, we had no track of time. It just flied."

Jenny said, "You are right. When you are busy, time flies."

"And if mannequins have work then they treat themselves as humans," said Ferry.

All were happy except Dish who was trying to make up with Attu. Saif called them.

"What happened Dish, why both of you are not joining us?"

"Saif, see Attu is angry with me. I was just joking and even Ice knew it."

"Had she not, I had to part with my clothes."

"Oh! As if you were always going to wear the same clothes."

"Those clothes were my favourite and I wanted to wear them for few more days."

Sitam said, "We all face the same problem. Some times we are dressed so badly that……………"

Ferry completed what Sitam couldn't describe.

Everybody laughed. Sitam was embarrassed.

"We are walking and speaking mannequins that are found nowhere else."

The discussion continued but Saif decided to take up this issue with Ice. The next day Ice went straight to Robin's cabin.

"Sir, there is something I want to talk about."

"Come, Ice, I was just about to call you. You have proved yourself on the very first day."

"I will do everything to save my job."

"You are permanent from today onwards."

"Thank you, Sir."

"Now, tell me what is there in your mind."

"Sir what I want is that dressing the mannequins should be in my hands. It is my request. You will have no complaints with my work."

"I know it. Yesterday, I saw you working on CCTV camera. I am quite pleased with you and can do as you wish."

"Thank you, Sir."

Ice left the cabin happily. She dressed all the mannequins the way she wanted. Attu was the last.

"So, Attu, I think you don't want your clothes to be changed?"

"Who said?"

"Why, yesterday you were upset with Dish. As far as I know these are your favourite clothes."

"Don't make me angry."

"What did I do?"

"First of all you came to me in the end that too without any clothes for me. All of them are looking so good. Please give me also a new look quickly. I want my wig to be changed as well."

Ice smiled and started to look for suitable clothes for Attu. One of her helper kept an eye on her for quite a long time.

"Ice, why were you smiling at the mannequin?"

"I was just thinking of giving it a new look. I always smile when I think."

The girl went away.

Attu said, "Now you seem to lie confidently."

"Any lie without a selfless motive, is not a lie."

"Is it some latest definition of a lie?"

"Yes, you can say it."

Attu was now completely ready.

Ferry whistled at him from a distance. "Hey, Attu you look completely different now."

Amber spoke, "Ice, now you will not have to worry about changing his clothes for a month."

"Why so?"

"He was not willing to part with his previous clothes since last ten days. This time he is looking very handsome so one month will be fine I guess."

"Why all of you always keep teasing me?"

"Because you are free."

This time Attu too laughed with them. Ice had a great difficulty holding back her laugh. Then Ice heard John and Jui calling her. She reached there and saw a small child adamant to buy something but his mother's choice was different.

"Madam, can I help you?"

"It's no use, my son is very stubborn. He never listens to anybody."

"Let me give it a try."

"As you wish."

"Hello, what is your name?"

He kept staring at Ice without any response.

"Should I show you some clothes?"

"No, I have already selected my clothes and I will take these only."

"That's good. But there are some clothes here also. It is no harm in giving it a look."

"You are only wasting your time."

"No problem, let's go."

"Okay."

"Ma'm I am taking him for a while, meanwhile you buy something for yourself."

"That's fine."

"Ice took the mischievous boy at a place where a heap of Teddy Bears was placed."

"Why you brought me here? I can't see any clothes here."

"Yes, you are right. There are no clothes; these Teddy Bears are my friends."

She picked up a Teddy and said, "He is their leader, see how fat he is. All are afraid of him and do you know why there is a scarf in his neck?"

"Why?"

"So that nobody sees his neck."

"Is there any problem with its neck?"

"No, but when he was being manufactured, he was very angry and he kept his neck stiffened. Since then his neck is like this."

Ice stiffened her neck and the boy giggled at her gesture. Ice played with him for a while and then she showed clothes to him. She lured him to wear the clothes of her choice and took him to his mother.

"Mummy, look at me. I am looking so smart."

"Yes, you are but you had selected……"

"This is better than what I choose."

She looked towards Ice, "You have done a wonderful job. He has been so difficult and your choice is even good."

"Thank you, Madam."

"From now on I will bring him here only."

While leaving, Ice kissed the boy. John and Jui watched everything.

John said, "This is something very bad. You never love us like this."

Jui said, "Yes, we are also as pretty as this child."

Before Ice could answer one of her co-employee approached her and said, "Ice, Mr. Robin wants to see you in furniture section."

When Ice reached there, Robin was already there with some people.

Robin said to her, "Ice, they are our very old customers and I want you to help them."

"Sure Sir, tell me what can I do?"

An old lady amongst them said, "We want complete furniture for one room. My granddaughter, along with her spouse, is coming from abroad for a month. They are rich people and we want no shortcomings on our part."

"If you can only tell me the likings of your granddaughter and her spouse along with the size of the room it will really be of great help for me."

They gave Ice all the required details. Ice pretended as she was listening to them very carefully, while she closed her eyes and visualized the room with all the furniture. They were still talking to her. She knew all these details are useless for her but she didn't want anyone to be suspicious so this was necessary. She helped them in buying the entire furniture. She told them the color that would suit the room.

Though they were not very happy but they didn't say anything. They left; Ice came back to her place.

Seeing Ice quiet, Amber and Ferry said, "What's the matter Ice? You are so quiet!"

"Yes, I doubt these people are not happy with my suggestions. I could feel what was going in their minds but they didn't say anything. I don't like to force my likings on the people. Were they forced to buy the furniture because of my powers? If it is so then I don't like it."

Ferry said, "You are blaming yourself for nothing. The whole idea was Attu's."

"What did you people do?"

"We transmitted some magical waves in them so that they buy the furniture suggested by you."

"This is not right."

"What's wrong in it? We have helped them. When the room is ready, they will be very happy."

"What, if it is the other way?"

"You once told us that the work done without any selfish motive always bring good results."

Ice was about to speak, she heard Attu, "Ice, come her quickly."

Ice saw a couple standing near Attu. The husband wanted to buy the shirt Attu was wearing but his wife was not agree with him. She pushed away his hand every time he tried to feel the shirt. Attu was in the centre.

"Ice, please do something, I am being hit for no reason."

Dish teased, "So now you got it. Ice, have you ever seen a mannequin being beaten up before?"

Before Ice could do something, Attu couldn't maintain his balance, as the couples were quarrelling with each other. He was about to fall when Ice came and held him.

"What are you doing? You were just about to hurt him."

"It is not some human who would get hurt?" said the lady.

"Excuse me Madam, but mannequins are more fragile than humans."

"She is right."

"Okay, now, tell me how can I help you?"

Ice arranged Attu properly and patted his hair affectionately.

"If this is the reward of what has happened just now, I would like to repeat it."

Ice didn't answer Attu but seeing this lady spoke, "You are taking care of this mannequin as if it has life."

"We remain in their company all the time so the affection develops."

The man said, "Moreover there is no risk involved in loving them as they always remain silent."

His wife gave him a cold stare. Ice managed to handle the situation. She got the same shirt but the color was of his wife's choice. So the problem was solved. Both left, happily.

Attu said, "I can never understand when a person knows his destiny after marriage why does he opt for one?"

Ice said, "Before marriage loneliness makes him suffer and after marriage company."

"Are you serious?"

"Do you really think one can be serious with you?"

"Fine, tell me Ice, will you marry?"

"I don't know. But if I find my love, I sure will. I think love is a blessing from God."

All the mannequins appreciated Ice's view.

"We all will pray for you to find a true love."

Sitam said, "You are in no danger."

"How come?"

"You can read his thoughts that will help you decide whether he really loves you or not?"

"No, for my love, I will not use my powers."

"You don't but we will surely do so."

They were busy in conversation when Gunjan interrupted, "Hey Ice, you don't want to go home? You still have not changed your clothes."

"It is only 4 p.m. now."

"Oh God! Are you lost? Did you forget, today is Aunty's birthday and we have taken half day to give her a surprise?"

Now it was Ice who was surprised, "Oh My God! Just give me five minutes to change."

Gunjan and Ice first went to the market to buy some sweets

and cake. When they reached home they found that Aunty had gone to the market. They quickly decorated the hall and arranged all the things on the table and pulled the lights off.

Aunty opened the door and was shocked to see the door unlocked, "Oh God! Who has opened the door? Ice comes late and nobody else has the keys of the house. I should find out who has dared to enter my house without my permission."

She entered the house talking to herself, just when the lights lightened every corner of the hall. Gunjan and Ice came in dancing.

"Happy Birthday, Aunty!"

"May you live for thousand years."

"So, you were behind all this, I got so scared."

"Don't lie, you were not scared. If there had been a thief, he must have had a good hand from you."

"You destroyed our whole plan. We had planned to scare you."

"How did you know about my birthday?"

"Ice told me."

Aunty looked curiously at Ice.

"Last weekend when you were cleaning your cupboard with me, I found an old greeting card."

"Thanks Ice. I had forgotten my birthday. I had started considering my life and my existence as meaningless."

"From now on, never think like this and here comes your gift."

"It was not needed."

Gunjan said, "You are right. I was telling Ice, it is not required, still she purchased it."

Sunaina opened it and found a bell with a very sweet tone.

"Aunty, now you don't have to come upstairs to call me.

You just ring this bell and I will be at your service. You can even ring it at night."

Tears ran down Sunaina's cheeks, "Even my own children have not cared this much."

"Only sweet talks will not do, you have to take us for dinner."

"First we will cut the cake."

"Both of you are crazy."

"Crazy people can only make you happy."

"Here you go; Ice has already admitted she is crazy."

The rest of the day passed pleasantly. In the night Saif didn't return home. Ice felt lonely without him. She was tired so she went off to sleep. In the morning, she woke up to Saif's call.

"Wake up Ice, it's morning."

Ice opened her eyes and asked, "Grandfather, are you leaving early today?"

"Yes Ice, the more I practise the better it is."

"So you will not talk to me even?"

"That is why I woke you up. Let's talk for sometime then I will leave. I hope you are not facing any problem in the Mall."

"Not at all. The Mall is a wonderful place and we are having a lot of fun over there."

"Yes, I know. All of them are also very happy. Instead of me they wait for you."

"I can't understand though all the mannequins are same but their natures are different."

"Why? Don't different humans have different nature?"

"It is true. But there is one or the other reason behind it. Their surroundings and brought up is also different. On the other hand the mannequins have got their thoughts with the help of the locket."

"You are right. After they came under the influence of the locket whoever touched or decorated them first, they got their characteristics from that person and moreover day by day they are learning new things."

"Though their thinking is pure but some bad habits….."

"Listen my dear, a person turns evil due to his or her selfish motives. But they don't have any motive to be selfish."

"Yes, grandfather, it is true. Selfishness robs a person's happiness and degrades him. That is why these mannequins are always happy."

"I think if we go on talking, we will get late."

Ice looked at the watch, "Yes, it is already late. I have to get ready quickly."

Ice went to have bath. When she came out, Saif had gone after arranging the room in order. There was a photo of Ice in the room that turned to Saif's photo whenever he was there. So that Ice could understand the presence of her grandfather.

"Thanks, grandpa. But I think if you keep doing all these work, it will make me lazy one day."

Ice was talking to herself when she heard Aunty's bell. Ice came down and saw Gunjan also there.

So it is you who ranged the bell. Why didn't you come upstairs, are your legs paining?"

"No, it's not my leg but my stomach."

"I can understand. I saw you eating the large chunk of cake last night."

"Oh dear, my stomach is not aching from over eating but from hunger."

"You didn't have breakfast?"

"Yesterday, Aunty told me the menu of today's breakfast."

"Oh! So this is the reason, a late comer like you came in so early."

"I am late while going and you are always late while returning back from there."

Aunty interrupted them, "What do you mean Gunjan?"

"Aunty, you don't know, she is so occupied in the Mall as if some party is going on. She takes extraordinary care of the mannequins. She always keeps decorating them. I think one day she will marry one of the mannequins."

Ice spoke in a serious tone, "Saying such things here is alright but don't say all this in the Mall."

"Why?"

"If the mannequins hear all this, they will be after me. I cannot marry all of them."

They had a hearty laugh. They had their breakfast. Both the girls left for the Mall.

Wiping the table Sunaina thought, "O God, I wish you would have blessed me with a daughter. I wonder why people don't feel happy on the birth of a girl child."

Gunjan and Ice had taken charge of their respective duties in the Mall. Ice was arranging clothes as some new clothes were to be displayed. After completing Ice went to look for some bangles as she wanted Dish and Ferry to wear them. She selected a bracelet for Dish when a beautiful girl came to her.

"Can I see this?"

"Sure Madam, this is for you."

"It is good but does not go with this dress."

She showed her dress to Ice.

"Your dress is very pretty but this bracelet really doesn't match with it."

Ice helped her with matching. Ice noticed everything she selected was quite expensive. If shown something cheap, she asked for something more attractive. Ice first thought of reading her mind but decided otherwise. She got herself busy with work. When the girl finally selected all the things a boy came in. Ice liked the couple. He showed his new clothes to the girl. Both were praising each other. Ice felt this behavior strange.

August who was standing not very far, commented, "You are thinking right, Ice. Both of them are making fool of each other. They don't love each other."

"Why?"

"It's simple. The boy is rich and just passing time with the girl, who is poor but wants her desires fulfilled."

"What will happen when the reality comes out?"

"They know world is like this only. There are all kinds of people in this world. One should have the ability to identify people."

Ice was uncomfortable watching them, so she left the place. Suddenly, she heard John crying.

Ice thought, "It seems John had fallen."

As she reached there she found a complete different picture. Jui was laughing loudly and John was murmuring in anger.

"You are absolutely fine John. Why did you cry? Why are you so angry?"

"What do you mean by absolutely fine? Come closer and have a look at me."

Ice went closer to it, "Oh! I think somebody has thrown water on you. There is a small pool on your feet."

"This is not water but urine."

"Urine! How?"

"See behind you."

Ice turned back, saw a lovely child looking at her. His clothes were also wet. Ice couldn't stop laughing.

"Hello, baby. Where is your mother?"

The child was still not able to speak. Instead he gestured on the other side. Ice carried him to his mother.

John shouted, "Ice, first get this mess cleaned. It's smelling horrible."

"Just wait for a minute. I will send somebody." Ice transmitted the message.

After a while everything was in order except John's mood. He was not talking to anybody. Jui tried her best to please him. Ice changed his clothes also. All the mannequins were making vain attempts to make him laugh. In the meantime an elderly person came in to buy clothes. His height was same as of John. He stood facing John.

Ice saw him and said, "Can I help you, Sir?"

"I want clothes of the size of this mannequin."

"Follow me, Sir."

"No, I will stay here only. You bring the clothes."

He was continuously staring at John, Ice asked, "Sir! Anything special about this mannequin?"

"You know I looked exactly like him when I was young. He will look like me when he is old."

"Right, Sir."

Saying this old man laughed loudly.

"Oh, you became serious. I was just joking. A man should always be in a jovial spirits."

"You really are a very nice person."

"No, I am just a short person." He laughed again.

"Height doesn't matter because you are big hearted. So you look happy."

"Thanks my child, you too have a nice heart. May God bless you with all your wishes."

"Now let me show you some clothes."

The old man selected many clothes but purchased only the ones Ice suggested.

"I never enjoyed shopping so much before."

"You will enjoy even more when you wear these."

"Just tell me. Don't you feel like laughing on my appearance?"

"You are just like my grandfather and why would I laugh at you?"

"What is the name of your grandfather?"

"Saif, Sir."

He was startled to hear the name, "You mean Saif, the magician? Are you the granddaughter of Saif?"

"Yes, do you know him?"

"Many years ago he………"

"Disappeared."

"Is he alive now?"

"No."

Tears rolled down his eyes as he said, "I am Manas Roy. Long ago, Saif and I studied together. He was not interested in studies. I became an advocate and he……… He was very hard working and pure hearted."

Wiping his tears, he said, "Here is my card, child. Whenever you need your grandfather, drop in without any hesitation."

He took his packet and left. Ice watched him going.

She sighed, "If only it was possible for me I wish you would see your friend."

In the night when Ice was about to sleep, she felt her grandfather's presence.

"What's the matter grandpa, you came in so late?"

"Yes, I went to see the mannequins and came to know that

you met Manas. Give me his address. I want to meet him. He will be very happy to see me."

"What are you saying? You know you cannot meet him."

"Why not? He is very brave and he will not be scared of me. We have many things to talk about."

"How will you manage to talk to him? He can only feel you but can't listen or see you."

In the excitement, reality slipped of Saif's mind. He calmed himself and looked depressed.

"Don't be upset, grandpa. If you wish to meet him tomorrow, I will go to his house and tell him the truth."

"No, Ice. I think it wouldn't be the right thing to do. Also the chants I am taming doesn't allow me to divert mind in other matters."

"You are tired, please rest for a while."

"No, I have to go. I may not be able to see you on regular basis. You take care of yourself."

After he left, Ice thought about the magic that was so important for her grandfather. Lost in these thoughts she fell asleep.

Ice was quiet happy with the mannequins. Now, the customers also knew her and approached her directly for help. Every type of people visited the Mall. Sometimes Ice was happy to see them, on other occasions their evil thoughts disturbed her. During such moments mannequins helped her.

It was quiet different as one day a pocket picker sneaked in the Mall. He stole purses of many people. There was chaos in the Mall. The security people closed the Mall and started to check the people. The mannequins told Ice about the thief. Ice was very upset to know that he did all this only to get her mother operated. If he is unable to collect the needed amount, chances of his mother's survival will almost be nil.

Ice was thinking of some way out to save this boy. She gathered some clothes and reached the boy, "The clothes that you had selected for yourself are available in your size. Should I get them billed?"

The boy surprisedly said, "See, I have…………"

Ice spoke in a low voice, "I know everything. While seeing the clothes you put all the purses in the clothes and meet me outside the Mall after an hour."

"Why are you helping me out?"

"Don't think otherwise, there is no time to think, be quick."

The boy agreed and left the Mall after getting checked up by the security people. In the Mall Ice deposited the purses pretending the thief had thrown the purses in the clothes being afraid of caught. After a while atmosphere seemed normal, Ice headed to see the boy outside the Mall.

"How do you know that purses were with me."

"The expressions on your face made it evident."

"I must say you are really a good observant. Sister, believe me, I don't have any other choice. My mother is very sick. I have to deposit the money for her operation."

I will go to the hospital with you to deposit the money."

"You don't even know me."

"Have faith in God. Meet me here only at 5.00 in the evening. I am Ice. Now I have to go back to work."

"I am Som. I will wait for you."

Ice went along with the boy in the evening. She deposited the required amount in the hospital.

The boy was employed in a factory and the owner had refused to give him any money in advance.

"Sister, I will return your money as soon as possible."

"It is not required Som, you just take good care of your mother."

Som was quiet. Ice left. Before this Som had only seen mean people in his life. This was difficult for him to believe.

The next day, Ice was alone on her way to work as Gunjan was not feeling well. Ice was waiting for her bus at the bus stop. An old car came to the stop and a boy asked Ice for an address. Ice was surprised as he was enquired the whereabouts of the Mall. Ice gave him the directions. While starting the car he asked, "If you are also going in the same direction I can drop you on the way."

Ice, who had not paid much of her attention to the boy now saw him. He was a charming boy who would draw any young girl's attention. He had curly hair and seemed to be from a well to do family. Ice started reading his mind.

"Perhaps I shouldn't have asked in this manner, what will she think of me? She must be thinking that I am trying to flirt with her."

Ice smiled to his thoughts and said, "Sure. I work there only."

"That's good."

Ice seated herself on the adjoining seat.

"Why are going to the Mall? If you have planned some shopping then you have to wait for a while."

"No, I am not going there to shop. I have to meet Mr. Robin. I want to show him some of my designs."

"He comes late."

"I have taken an appointment with him for this time."

"Then, sure he will be there."

There were hardly any talks afterwards. Reaching the Mall both thanked each other and went their ways. After sometime, one of the colleagues of Ice told her that Mr. Robin wants to see her.

Ice found the same boy in Mr. Robin's cabin, "Yes, Sir."

"Come in Ice, meet Mr. Mani. He is here with some of his designs that seem to be pretty good to me."

"Hello! Mr. Mani. I never expected second meeting so soon."

"Have you already met?"

"This morning he gave me a lift."

"Mr. Mani, she is the girl I was talking about. If she likes the designs, you can expect a healthy order."

"Sir, if you have already selected some designs then........."

"No, I want you to take the decision."

Mani pushed the file towards Ice.

Looking at file she said, "Mr. Mani can you leave this file with me for day?"

"I'm sorry, no designer will do that."

"You are right, I need some time."

Robin interrupted, "Tomorrow the Mall is off. Both of you can meet somewhere and spend time on the selection. You can also come to my place."

"If this is so, then Ice can come to my factory where I can show her some other designs besides the catalogue."

"It's fine. You give me your address and I will see you tomorrow."

"Ice, you can place an order on all the designs you like without my approval. Moreover, I will be out of town for the next two days."

The discussion was over. She noticed Mani walking with the help of a stick though there seemed to be no problem. Ice was thinking of him when she heard Amber and Ferry.

"Ice, can you come here, please?"

Ice reached there, "What is it Ferry?"

"See, the couple in blue shirt and sari standing behind us."

"What is so special about them?"

They both love each other immensely but can't express their feelings."

"So, you know them."

"Yes, they are visiting this place from last one year."

"Why don't they express each other?"

"Both work for the same company. The girl is on a higher post which makes the boy hesitant to propose; on the other hand girl is too shy to say anything. You must do something."

"Let me try."

Ice went closer to them, "Can I help you people?"

"Sure. A friend of the Madam is getting married. We are confused about the gift."

"You can gift a couple watch or a beautiful clock for the room. Here you can have a look."

Both of them started looking. Meanwhile, Ice asked the boy, "When you love her why don't you tell her?"

"How do you know?"

"That`s not the matter of concern, will you propose her or not?"

"She is my boss. I don't have courage to approach her."

"I have an idea."

Ice told something in his ear to which he agreed. After sometime when they got their gifts packed, Ice came with a showpiece and said, "You can also buy this pair of parrots, it will enhance your love and understanding."

The boy said, "We are not married."

"So what, one day you will marry. Should I get it billed Madam?"

The girl didn't answer but their hearts were beating fast.

Ice made her last effort, "Madam, please say something otherwise he will think that you don't want to marry him."

Suddenly she spoke out, "No, it's not like that."

The boy felt positive now, "So, can we have it?"

She just smiled, "O.K."

Ice made a gesture towards the boy and went away to get it packed.

"I was willing to say this to you for a long time but didn't have the courage."

"I have been waiting for this moment for the last one year."

"Sorry, Madam."

"Will you still call me Madam?"

The boy removed a ring out of his pocket and delicately placed it in her finger.

"When did you get this?"

"I bought it one year ago with the feeling that either it will be yours or nobody's."

"You used to bring it to the office daily?"

"Yes."

"Shyam, you are crazy."

"Radha's Shyam has to be crazy."

"Thank God! At least my name came on your lips."

"Let's go now."

Ice called them, "Madam, what about taking your gift?"

Both stopped, "Oh! Sorry. We just forgot."

"I will always treasure this as it brought us together."

"No, Radha, the real credit is hers. We will never forget her kind gesture."

Ice saw them leaving. All the mannequins were happy too and they made great noise.

"We should party tonight."

"Yes, it will be great fun."

"What fun? Ice cannot come and these days Saif too visits us for a short time."

"Ice, all of us are very good at dancing. You will enjoy it."

"I know but it is not possible."

Ferry said, "O.k. Ice, tell us. If you fall in love with somebody what will you do?"

"I will tell him immediately."

All the mannequins laughed.

Amber said, "We will wait for that moment, Ice."

Next day, when Ice was descending stairs Aunty asked, "Where are you going, Ice? Isn't it off today?"

"Yes Aunty, though the Mall is closed but my boss has asked me to visit a garment factory to select some designs."

Aunty said in an irritated tone, "They pay you the same salary but work is assigned for the weekend too."

"Don't worry, Aunty, I will be back soon."

Aunty asked for breakfast.

"No, Aunty I am not hungry now."

Ice reached the given address. It was a narrow street in the old city. She knocked at the door, Mr. Mani opened the door for her.

"Oh! It's you! Please come in."

"It seems you are surprised to see me as if I have dropped in suddenly."

"No, it's not like that. I didn't expect you so early."

"Is it a problem that I have dropped in so early?"

"No, no. Have a seat please. Actually, I usually work till late hours and so I wake up late. Just give me five minutes to get fresh."

He went away. Ice saw her surroundings. There was a hall

like room having three small store rooms. Ice felt strange seeing only one stitching machine there. On one table there were clothes with tailors working tools. There was a rack on which stitched clothes were placed. There was a press on one side and a cupboard with many files. The rest of the cupboards were closed. The room gave the impression that work was done regularly.

In the meanwhile, Mani returned, "Sorry, I hope, I have not wasted much of your time."

"No, it hardly matters. Now tell me % Is this your factory?"

"Why, is there something wrong?"

"Yes, you say it a factory but I see only one sewing machine here. It is strange."

"The fact is that once I cut the clothes, I get the stitching done on job work basis."

Ice could read his lie. She started reading his mind.

He was thinking, "How can I tell her that I manage everything myself. If I tell her that I work for 16 hours a day, she will think that I am a crazy man."

Ice decided to explore him further, "Let's have a look at the designs."

"Sure."

Mani showed her new designs, some ready samples and some fabrics. Ice quite liked his work then with her magical powers, she selected the designs and gave him a bulky order. Ice also suggested some changes which were appreciated by Mani too.

"I never had an idea of you being so good with designing."

Ice only managed to pass a smile.

"You be seated, I will bring something to eat."

"But it is ………."

Please don't say no. I know both of us are hungry."

He went for fetching breakfast, Ice decided to know whether it will be a long term business relation with him or not? How will her relation with Mr. Mani be after one year? So Ice closed her eyes when she opened her eyes, she was very nervous.

What she had seen was unbelievable. She saw herself in the arms of Mr. Mani.

"How can it be possible? I have never dreamt of any guy even in my wildest dreams….. So is he my life partner? No, no. I remember Mom always use to say that when Mr. Right will come in my life I will feel something different in my heart. But I don't feel anything for him. I may be wrong."

Mani came back and Ice disconnected herself from her thoughts.

He looked at Ice, "Has something happened?"

"No. Why?"

"You are looking a bit frightened."

"There is nothing to frighten me."

"You bet, there is."

"What?"

"Lizard."

"Really."

"Yes, I have heard girls are very afraid of lizards. In my room they crawl on the floor too."

"I thought you won't talk anything else except your work."

"Yes. When it is business, I talk only business, but for now we are finished with it."

"Do your friends have the same opinion about you?"

"I have no friends. Frankly speaking I never felt the need for it. I feel happy whenever I create a unique design."

"You are quite different."

"I know. Will you like to have something else?"

"No, thanks. I must leave now."

"Will you have a coffee? I am very good at it."

"Later, Mr. Mani. I have eaten too much for now."

"As you wish. You can call me Coke, that's my nick name."

Ice took leave with a smile. Ice noticed today he was not holding the stick. She got confused. She decided neither to tell of the meeting with Coke to her grandfather, nor she will meet him again.

Next day at the Mall her co-helper Mita met Ice. She looked very disturbed.

"What has happened Mita? Why has your face has lost its charm?

"Please, Ice, I need your help."

"I will help you but first tell me something."

"Ice, a boy is following me for the last three months."

"What does he want?"

"He says, he wants to marry me."

"You don't like him?"

"I don't trust him, Ice."

"Any specific reason for this?"

"I am a girl from a simple family. I know neither I am beautiful nor smart with my talks like you. I also don't even know to handle people while talking. Then why should a handsome and rich boy like to marry me?"

"It is possible you are mistaken."

"If my doubts prove to be true it will only bring disrepute to my family."

"You call him here once."

"He will be here in a short while."

"Let me think of something. You call me whenever he comes."

Mita got busy with her work. Ice asked for the help of mannequins.

"Can you people do something in this matter?"

Everybody started speaking one after the other.

"Ice, Mita is right. The guy is making fool of her."

"Why so?"

"A truth exposed by Mita's father caused him a great damage. Now he wants to take revenge by disrupting his image."

"Oh God! people can go to any limits."

"You have to save Mita."

"How?"

"We don't know but whenever he comes to the Mall, he cheaply stares the beautiful girl. He has a very dirty mind."

Ice thought for a while then she came up with a plan with the mannequins. Mita liked her plan very much. After sometime the boy came in the Mall.

"What do you think?" he asked Mita.

"Listen Rahul, I have something very important to tell you."

"What can be more important than our relationship?"

"There is one of my friends who works with me. The moment she saw you, she has fallen in love with you."

"But I………."

"I know this. I want you to just meet her once. Still if you find me more suitable than her I will marry you."

"If you so want it, I will meet her for your sake."

Mita told him the meeting place as decided. He left the place happily.

"Ice, you are taking a big risk for me."

"Don't worry, I will be fine."

Ice left the Mall early. She got her best outfit and shoes. Making an excuse to Aunty she reached a beauty parlour. Once she finished, it seemed difficult to recognize her. She reached the meeting point where Rahul was waiting for her.

She stood right behind him.

"Hello, Rahul. Sorry, for being late."

Rahul was angry, "I have never waited so long for anybody in my life, instead girls use to wait…….."

The next words melted in his mouth. His eyes were set on Ice who was looking so pretty for which everybody was looking at her.

"Yes, you were saying something."

"I never knew I was here to meet a fairy."

"Thanks. Can I sit?"

"Oh! I just forgot everything after seeing you."

"Thanks."

"I cannot believe you work in a Mall."

"No, I work in a bank."

"Anyway, why did you want to meet me?"

Ice didn't answer a single question straightway. Moreover she avoided the mention of Mita and the Mall. After the meal she deliberately spilled ice-cream on her dress and asking excuse to clean herself she went home. She again visited the parlour to be back into her normal looks so that no one doubts.

Next day Ice saw Rahul outside the Mall. He was looking upset. She knew that he was waiting for Mita. Ice had already explained Mita everything over phone.

Gunjan said, "Ice, is he the same boy?"

"Yes, now you know what you have to do?"

"Yes, I know, hats off to your courage."

Laughing, both of them went inside. Rahul's eyes caught Mita. He approached her eagerly."

"Mita, yesterday your friend came to meet me."

"No, yesterday boss didn't permit her to go, so she was in the Mall only."

"You are lying."

"Why should I?"

"Why not? Come with me."

Mita came with Gunjan.

"Sorry, you were not with me yesterday."

"I never said so."

"Who was she?"

"I don't know."

"You were with her for such a long time but never asked her name?"

"I forgot everything as I saw her."

"Fine then, leave me alone."

"Let's go for the duty Mita."

Both left him standing in a confused state of mind. Once inside Gunjan told Ice, "You should have seen his face."

Before Ice could reply Attu's message came, "Ice, be careful, that boy is coming inside to find you."

Ice said, "Look Gunjan we shall not discuss this issue any more."

Then she got busy with her work. Rahul searched her for two hours. She kept avoiding him with the help of the mannequins.

"Oh! I am tired of running here and there."

Dish said, "Feel free, he has left."

"Thanks God."

"He will come back."

Attu teased, "You have turned him crazy."

Ferry said, "Moreover, he is a good looking, handsome and rich guy."

Ice said, "So according to you these are the norms to get married."

"See, all of us are unmarried and you tell us what to look in for a suitable boy?"

"You people are just trying to fool me? I will marry only when I feel that love for someone."

"Love…."

"No more discussions please. A lot of time has already been wasted since morning. Let's start with our routine work."

Sitam said, "Fine Ice, you come this side. Somebody is here."

Ice saw a beautiful girl standing beside Sitam. She was looking at his clothes but her mind was somewhere else. It seemed she was there for something else than clothes.

"You are thinking right Ice. She is looking for a boy."

"Is it? So our Mall is used for such activities as well?"

"Don't take it lightly, she is looking really upset."

"Tell me what the problem is?"

"She is the only child of her rich parents. They want her to marry but she doesn't believe in love though she is nice hearted."

"If she doesn't want to marry why is she looking for a boy?"

"Her parents had given her six months time to get a suitable boy for her otherwise she has to marry according to their will. Tomorrow is the last day."

"What kind of boy, is she looking for?"

"Who being a husband only plays the role of a husband."

"You mean a husband in front of the society and a stranger in personal life?"

"If she marries a wrong person her life will be in a mess."

Ice's mind was working at a quick pace. She closed her eyes and thought. After a while she opened her eyes with a smile. She approached the girl.

"Can I help you Madam?"

"No thanks. I am not looking for clothes."

"Fine, then you must look at this locket. It will suit you."

Though she was not willing, Ice gave the locket in her hand. Both of them looked at the locket.

"You are looking quite upset. I think you didn't like the locket."

While saying this Ice took the locket back and pretended to see her palms.

"Hey Madam, you are going to be married soon."

The girl was taken aback, "How do you know?"

"I know palmistry. I can see that the boy will be of your choice."

Suddenly, the girl's eyes lit up, "You can surely help me."

"I don't understand."

"Can you accompany me for sometime out of this Mall?"

"Yes, why not?"

After a while they were sitting in a Coffee House. Her name was Shalu , she told Ice everything that Sitam had said earlier. During the course of their discussion, Ice told Shalu about the boy who came to the Mall to steal wallets. Ice told Shalu the whole truth about Som, Ice called Som to the Mall so that she could take the help of the mannequins also in this matter.

Som came in the evening. Ice told him all the details about Shalu and their conversation.

"Look sister, I don't agree to this. It's like deceiving her parents."

"You are thinking the wrong way, Som. If Shalu marries a wrong person then she and her parent's life will be destroyed."

Ice left Shalu and Som alone. Som told Shalu everything. He also told her that he is getting married with her only because of Ice, otherwise he had decided never to get married. Shalu liked his truthfulness.

After a while, Ice came to them, "So what has been decided by you two?"

"Right now I am going to meet Shalu's parents."

"That's good. I hope your compromises will lead you to an happy ending."

Next morning all the mannequins praised Ice.

"Hey Ice, you have done a miracle."

"What is it?"

"I knew it well for which I asked your help."

"Now please stop praising me, all the credit goes to the magical powers of grandpa."

"How come?"

"When I closed my eyes and called for help, I could see Somu and Shalu playing with a baby. Immediately I knew what to do."

Dish said, "You know things just by seeing but Attu can't understand even if you instruct him."

"Why are you people always teasing Attu?"

"Just listen to what he did, you will automatically understand."

"Saif is also not here, what if anything goes wrong?"

Ice stopped her work and asked, "Will somebody tell me what has happened?"

Gunjan was standing besides her, "What happened Ice? Is something wrong?"

"Nothing, you just arrange these clothes, I will be back shortly."

She went to Ferry and started fixing her clothes, "Ferry, what is it, what are you talking about? I can't understand anything."

"Attu has hidden a puppy in the store room since last night."

"What? A puppy, how did he come into the Mall?"

"We don't know the details, perhaps it was in a box. He is too small to open his eyes also."

"Where is he right now?"

"Attu has hidden him behind the boxes so that nobody can see."

"It is not fair, he can die."

Ice and the rest of the mannequins were communicating through mind waves. Ice bought a bottle of milk and fed the puppy. While Ice was doing this, Saif came.

"How are you Ice?"

"Grandpa! It is nice to see you after so many days. Are you thorough with your work?"

"No, I have come midway."

"Any specific reason?"

"Yes, Ice. You know the mannequins work with the power of the locket. Usually I transit them power once a week but yesterday I thought, I will not be able to come for at least a month. So, I decided to expose them to more powerful rays but something went wrong."

"Didn't the mannequins receive power?"

"What I wished did happen but something else was also done along with it."

"I do not understand anything you are saying."

"The time I was exposing them to the rays of the locket I didn't notice the puppy in Attu's hands."

"You mean to say that puppy also got the powers?"

"Yes, Ice. Now this puppy also possesses many magical powers. I want you to keep it with you. You can talk to him as you do with mannequins. He will also understand you. Though he will look like an ordinary dog but he work like a human being."

"Now what should I do?"

"Take it home in a bag and don't show it to anybody, otherwise everybody will ask for it."

Grandpa left but Ice was quite upset. She knew that Sunaina had no liking for dogs. It was a problem for her. She will never allow her to keep the dog. She put the puppy in a bag and got busy with her work. She was confused about the puppy.

Attu said, "You don't tell Sunaina and moreover, she never comes upstairs."

"How long I shall be able to do like this? Though she doesn't come up what if the dog goes downstairs? I will be in the Mall and he will be at home. I shall not be able to concentrate on my work."

"Then let him be here only. All you have to do is to make arrangement for its meals. Leave the rest to me."

Dish said, "You keep quiet Attu. You have already doubled our troubles with your brilliance."

"I didn't do it deliberately."

"You are lying? We all told you to not to take him out of the box."

"I had never seen an animal before."

"The same was with us."

Ice was angry, "Stop it now. Instead of helping me out, you are fighting."

All became quiet but no one had suggestion. In the

meantime, Mr. Robin called Ice into his cabin. Mani was also there.

Robin said, "Look Ice, Mr. Mani has completed all the orders. All his designs are selling like hot cakes. What do you think?"

"You are absolutely right, Sir. Now we can place a bulk order."

"Fine. Mr. Mani wants you to select all the designs."

"Sir, this......."

"I know this is my work. Your team work has given wonderful results, so I shall wish the same to be continued."

Mani said, "Excuse me, if Miss Ice is not willing then you decide."

"No, no, this is not the matter. Today, I want to leave early."

Robin told, "So, what's the problem. You can accompany Mr. Mani right now."

Ice thought quickly, "This will be fine. I will be back after changing my clothes."

Ice had already thought of keeping the puppy with Mani. She knew he will not refuse.

On their way Ice remained quiet. She didn't know how to put the idea before Mani. Mani opened the door, offering her to sit and went to prepare coffee.

"Here it is!"

"Oh! You are making coffee? I thought...."

"You are looking upset so I thought coffee may help."

"Thanks! How did you know?"

"It's all on your face. If it is something personal then it is fine otherwise I can help you."

"Will you help me?"

"Yes. You can trust me."

"The problem is not something to talk about, rather it needs to be seen."

Mani was unable to understand her. In the meantime, Ice produced the puppy from the bag who had now opened his eyes.

"Oh! he is very cute. So, this is your problem."

"Yes, I found it in the Mall. How it got inside is still a mystery. Neither I want to lose it nor I can keep it with me because Aunty will not allow."

"Then, let it be with me."

Ice lit up, "Thank you Mr. Mani. You have solved my problem."

"I only help friends."

When Ice looked at him, he had a naughty smile on his face.

Ice also decided to continue the sarcasm, "Then, let's be friends. When there is no way out, you have to be friends even with an ass…."

Both laughed.

"Mr. Mani, coffee is nice."

"I am Coke."

"I am Ice."

"Okay, I got it. Let's discuss about work."

Thus both of them spent a lot of time discussing the designs.

Suddenly, Ice looked at the watch, "Oh! It's very late, I didn't realize the time. I must go now."

"If there is no other trouble then a person can work comfortably."

"Now you are pulling my legs."

"No, no, I was just trying to suggest that your important

work for the evening is now my responsibility, so let's have a dinner out."

"Aunty will prepare…."

"Inform her over the phone."

Ice started thinking and decided to read Coke's mind.

Coke was thinking, "I don't know how to ask girls out? I have never done such thing so far."

Coke said, "If you are comfortable then I can drop you home."

"No, this is not the reason; the reason is that I have never been out with a boy."

"Believe me, same is the case with me. I was thinking whether my way of asking you out was right or not?"

Ice smiled at his innocence. She informed Sunaina that she will be late for dinner.

"Let's go now."

Patting the puppy she said, "First we must feed him."

Coke brought milk and Ice fed the puppy.

"What's its name, Ice?"

"I've not thought about it."

"I have got a company now so I am very happy. Why not we name him Khushi?"

"It's a nice name."

At dinner, Coke spoke the most while Ice just listened to him carefully. She thought as she has no feelings for Coke so there is no harm in meeting him. In two meetings nothing of that sort had happened so she need not be afraid of him. On the other hand, Coke was not even aware of the feeling of being in a girl's company, so love was a far fetched thing.

"It was nice being with you."

"See you started being formal again."

"It's in my nature. I want to ask you something."

"Go ahead."

"Whenever you go outside, you always keep this stick with you though you don't require one. Why is it so?"

"Is it doing me any harm?"

"Yes, people think that there is some problem in your feet for which girls also avoid you."

"You have just given the answer yourself."

"So you do so to keep the girls away?"

"When I was in college, girls used to tease me a lot. I didn't have any fetish for fashionable girls. I got this idea while traveling when I saw a boy with a stick. After the college vacations got over I also started to keep a stick. When asked, I told that I had an accident and the stick became permanent feature."

"Did this solve your problem?"

"Absolutely. Now not only girls but boys also stopped teasing me."

"Why do you still keep this stick?"

"It's just a habit now, nothing else."

After this there were no special talks. Many days passed. During these days Coke and Ice never met but Ice used to call Coke to know about Khushi. The dog always followed Coke. Coke was surprised to know how easily Khushi understood him. Coke was not aware of his magical powers to understand human language but Khushi sometimes got upset when Coke was unable to understand him.

Ice was having a nice time in the Mall with her friends. Something or the other kept coming up and they solved the issue.

Everything was going on smoothly as one day Mita approached Ice in the Mall.

"Are you alright, Mita?"

"There is a big problem, Ice."

"What are you afraid of?"

"Not me, it's you who is in danger."

"Me? Why?"

"I have told Rahul that you are the same girl who met him."

"Why did you do so?"

"I was helpless Ice. He came to my house with two bad guys and threatened to kill my father. I had no other way out."

She started weeping.

"Don't cry, Mita. I can understand."

"You helped me out and I have put you in trouble."

"Did he say something?"

"He can drop in anytime to meet you."

"You don't worry, I will handle him."

Though Ice cooled down Mita but she had no idea for what to do?

August said, "Whatever has happened is very bad."

Jui who was least talkative said, "Outside the Mall, even we can't help you Ice?

Sitam said, "You should ask for Saif's help."

"No, he is busy with something important. I won't trouble him with this."

Ice and Mannequins were busy in discussion when Rahul came in from nowhere. He was standing in front of Ice.

"Yes, Sir. How can I help you?"

"Ice, you very well know why I am here."

Ice fearlessly answered, "Yes, I know. If you think that after threatening Mita you can repeat the same with me, then you are wrong."

"You deceived me."

"What did you do with Mita?"

"I wanted to take revenge."

"What is her fault in this?"

"Not hers. It was her father."

"Mita was not responsible for all that. You had planned to ruin an innocent girl. I was just helping my friend out."

"I admit I was wrong and am ready to repent for that."

"Oh! Really. Perhaps, for which you went to threaten Mita."

"I had no other way to meet you. If you just give me one chance, I will change myself for you."

"Look, Mr. Rahul I am not going to be convinced."

"Please believe me."

"Right, now it is my working time so you must leave."

"I am leaving now but I will see you again."

Rahul left leaving Ice upset. She was well aware that it was not easy to get rid of him.

Jenny said, "Ice, don't be upset. He didn't have any bad intentions. He will not hurt you."

"I know Jenny but such type of crazy lovers are unpredictable. Their minds and thoughts keeps fluctuating with time."

Ferry said, "I agree with Ice. We have to find a solution."

Attu said, "We can erase his memory of your meeting with him from his brain."

"Is it possible?"

"Yes, all of us in the Mall can do this."

"It's a good idea."

"No, I don't think it will be right."

Ice said, "Why Dish?"

"This will again draw his attention to Mita. These are the

only memories due to which he is trying to change himself. If we erase them he will be the same person again."

"I have not given any thought to this aspect."

"Ice, if you listen to Attu you shall always be get half knowledge."

"I have only told what I thought will be right."

"Please, don't start it again. Let me think."

Ice got busy with the work but was upset. In the evening Coke called.

"Hello, Ice! How are you?"

"Hello, I am fine. Tell me."

"I have come up with some designs. I wanted you to meet Khushi also. May be from tomorrow you have no time."

"Why?"

"You forgot? From tomorrow a sale is being organized in your Mall. There will be quite a rush."

"Oh! Yes. It just skipped my mind. I will just inform Robin Sir."

"I have already spoken to him. I am waiting outside in car so be quick."

When Ice reached at Coke's place, Khushi came running and jumped into Coke's lap. Coke patted him. Kushi saw Ice and barked a little. He was asking about Ice. Ice understood his language but it seemed Coke could also understand his gestures.

"Khushi, meet Ice, she is a friend of mine. It was she who brought you here."

Khushi barked, "I want to know from where did she bring me?"

Ice thought she should talk to Khushi but not in front of Coke.

"Coke, no coffee today?"

"Why not? I left home early today. You sit and I shall bring something to eat and milk. Khushi's biscuits are also finished. If you don't want to be alone you can accompany me."

"No, I'm fine here and moreover Khushi shall give me company. I shall try to develop a friendship with him."

Khushi kept looking at her continuously. When Coke had left, Ice extended her hand to Khushi.

"Can we be friends?"

Khushi barked, "Yes, but first tell me from where did you get me?"

"I have brought you from the Mall where I work."

"Can you understand what I say or you just have a wild guess as sometimes Coke does?"

"I can understand what you say."

Khushi jumped excitedly, "Say it again. I always thought that no human being could ever understand my language."

"What you think is right, Khushi. Animals and humans don't understand each other's language. It depends on gestures only."

"I can understand and you too can listen to me."

"Because both of us are blessed with some magical powers. This is the reason you can think and work like humans."

"From where did we have these powers?"

Ice told Khushi about Grandpa and the Mall. Khushi got all the answers to his questions.

"Is Coke aware of this?"

"No."

"Then we cannot talk in front of him?"

"We can. You shall get your answers in your mind without me speaking. In the Mall, I talk to the mannequins in the same manner. Now tell me, are you happy here?"

"Yes. Coke is a very nice person. He takes good care of me. Though he doesn't allow me to do some work as he thinks I am a mere dog."

"Don't worry, you are quite small. When you grow up, he will have confidence in you."

Realizing, Coke is back, Ice became quiet. Seeing Khushi in Ice's lap, Coke said, "So you two are friends now. Ice, he is very intelligent and understands whatever I say though I sometimes fail to reciprocate."

Ice just passed a smile. Coke offered some eatables to Khushi and he left Ice's lap. Giving her coffee, Coke asked, "Now tell me, what is the problem?"

"What are you talking about?"

"Something is worrying you. Today you are lost somewhere else. You smiled only when you saw Khushi. Can I help you in some way?"

"No, there is nothing."

"So, we are just formal friends?"

"If I tell you all about this you shall be upset with me."

"I promise, I will not be. Now tell me."

Ice told the whole episode of Mita and Rahul.

"I never knew, you do all such things as well, though your plan was very good."

"Still everything has gone wrong."

"You tell the boy that you are in love with somebody else."

"You don't know Rahul, he will not believe what I say."

"Then you make Rahul meet with some boy."

"Who, I don't know anybody."

"A friend in need is a friend indeed."

Ice got what he was trying to say, "You!"

"Why? Is there something wrong with me?"

"He will trouble you. He can even try to kill you."

"I am not some kind of vegetable whom he shall cut and throw away."

Ice didn't reply as she was thinking something else.

Silence prevailed for sometime. Then Coke said, "You should agree with me."

"Yes, but with slight modification."

"I can't get you."

"I shall tell Rahul that I love you but you don't want to marry me."

"How shall you explain reason behind this?"

"I shall say that you think that I want to marry you because I pity you."

"What pity?"

"As your leg was hurt while rescuing me."

"Hey Ice, you should be a writer."

"Thanks."

"Now, you have to admit my stick not only helps me but my friends also."

Both were smiling. Ice and Coke chalked out a solid plan for Rahul. Ice involved Mita and Gunjan too. For the next week Ice remained very busy. It was the first sale in the Mall after she joined. Mall's stores were brimming with stock. Robin issued instructions to keep the Mall open for maximum hours. To make it more spacious, Ice arranged mannequins in two halves. When Rahul called Ice, she told him about her busy schedule. She also told him someone was already there in her life.

The fifteen day long sale exhausted Ice. It was not only because of work but the mannequins also kept her busy with the customers. Sometimes Ice was able to help while at times she failed to do so. After sale was over, she took two days off. She was relaxing in her room. She was thinking with her eyes open.

"What's the use of taking a leave? I am not sick but I have no one to speak my heart out? If grandpa would have been here he could have understood my feelings."

The very moment Saif was there, "So, you were thinking about me?"

Ice was excited to have Saif beside her.

"When did you come grandpa? I have so many things to tell you."

"Is there any trouble?"

"No, there is none but whatever is happening at the Mall I have nobody to share with. Then I feel……."

"Okay, I understand."

"I am also very angry with you. So many days have gone, you never thought about me. Nor you came to see me."

"All your anger shall vanish when you see the present I have brought for you."

"I don't want anything from you, grandpa."

"Alright then."

"What do you mean?"

"Just look behind you."

Ice turned. Her eyes were spread wide. Was it a dream or reality? Her grandpa was sitting on a chair. She was able to see him.

Her eyes became numb. She kept on looking at him. When Saif put his hand on her head, she couldn't keep her tears back.

After some time she said, "You have brought me the most expensive gift on this earth."

"I was always worried about you."

"I am perfectly fine. Can everyone see you now, what sort of powers have you obtained?"

"I will answer these questions later on but as far as seeing me is concerned it depends on me. Only the person I wish can see me or hear me. I don't want to come in front of everyone."

"Why, grandpa?"

"It is not needed, Ice. Now tell me what has happened so far? Today the Mall is open, why are you at home? Is there any confrontation with the mannequins?"

"No, grandpa it is really nice being with them. There was a sale going on for the past fifteen days and we had a lot of fun."

"Tell me in detail."

"I have seen a lot in the last fifteen days. Different types of people in this world. Some have sacrificing nature while others are affected by hatred. On the second day of sale there were two couples in the Mall. Attu told me about them. They were recently married. The boy loved his wife very much but the girl was in love with someone else before their marriage. She had plans of running with her lover on that night. She came to the mall making an excuse that she has to meet one of her friend."

"Does the boy has any idea about his wife?"

"He will doubt only if he would know anything. He bought everything she wished for. Her happiness was everything for him."

"The second couple?"

"There story was altogether opposite. Here, the husband was dishonest. They were married for 10 years. The wife loved her husband from heart while he was involved with someone else. He wanted to poison her eventually. But when she came to know about this, she decided to leave the house without saying a word."

"Both the stories were completely different."

"There was one similarity."

"What?"

"The reasons may differ but in both the cases the wives left."

"Why didn't you do something?"

"We gave it much thought but the circumstance didn't allow us to do anything. That day I and mannequins realized our helplessness."

"I don't know about their consequences."

"Whatever happened even we didn't imagine but we tried to help a little for which everything was okay."

"How?"

"The cheat husband got a letter from his wife after she left, only then he realized that his true happiness was with her. He got furious with himself. He searched her like a mad person but couldn't find her."

"How did you help?"

"He came to the Mall to refresh the moments he spent with her in the Mall. We saw change in him. We knew his wife was in an old age home as there was a call from there on her mobile when she was in the Mall."

"How did you convey him?"

"It was a difficult task. I went to him and said — Some days back you were here with your wife."

"Yes, why are you asking?"

"I saw your wife in an old age home. I don't know why she is there but……. Later nothing was needed on my part. He took the address and left."

"He might come back to thank you."

"Yes, both the couples came."

"Where did you find the second couple?"

"This is it grandpa. I was also astonished to see both of them very happy. They invited me at their house. There I got to know that both the wives were childhood friends. While they were leaving the house they met in a train. Both recognized and advised each other to return home. One girl was alone as the other was accompanied by her lover. The next morning when she woke up, her lover was gone with her luggage, jewellery and money. The true friend is one who stands with you in sufferings."

"Then both of them must have left for old age home?"

"Exactly! When one husband reached there to take his wife back the other girl also became hopeful that her husband might also forgive her."

"If a person mends his mistake within time it makes his life smooth."

"Today both the couples are happy. I am unable to decide, who is greater? The one who improves or the one who forgives?"

"It doesn't require so much thinking, Ice. It is the humble nature of the person which makes him great and there is one more reason they realized their mistakes only after seeing the greatness of their partners."

"It's fine, I don't know how people can be so sacrificing."

"A true love knows no boundaries as everything is possible in love and war."

"Grandpa, love, I remember Mr. Robin's nephew, Mantu, got crazy about me. He made it difficult for me to work in the Mall."

"Why didn't you tell Mr. Robin?"

"How could I complain against a child?"

"Oh, you are talking about a child; I thought he was a young man."

"Mantu is a grown up boy but from brain he is an eight year old child. Sometimes back he used to accompany Mr. Robin. I used to answer his innocent questions. One day he told me, all of his friends have girl friends. Can I be his girl friend? I said yes. I had no idea, he will take it so seriously. Later he started proposing me regularly for marriage. In the Mall all used to laugh at him. My friends also teased me by calling him as my husband. According to mannequins he was the best option available for me as I wanted a truthful person."

Saif laughed at everything. Ice got angry.

"Grandpa, you are also laughing? I will not tell you anything now."

"Fine, I will not laugh. Tell me further?"

"One day he came and informed me about his birthday in the coming week and proposed me to get engaged on that day. I was not sure about what to do."

"You should have asked for Mr. Robin's help."

"I told him but he got angry with me and said that I was responsible for Mantu's state of mind."

"It is rightly said that sometimes being nice also can trouble you."

"Grandpa, the way mannequins helped me was something that even humans couldn't have done."

"What?"

"As the birthday of Mantu was approaching, I was getting more and more tensed. Mannequins knew it. They made a plan without my knowledge. The mannequins came to know somehow Mantu was not like this from the very birth. He turned like this after a brain injury. It was two years ago. The mannequins had the power to heal him by striking the same spot on his brain. But it was only possible if Mantu touched one of the mannequins. They planned as the opportunity comes one of the mannequins will fall over him and hit the affected part of his brain."

"Mannequins could have been hurt in this process."

"That is why they didn't involve me in their plan. After three days of observing Mantu they got the opportunity. Mantu was fixing Jenny's locket when Mall was about to close. Seeing nobody around August pushed him. Before he could balance himself he fell on Sitam and Sitam stroked his head. He fell unconscious."

"I hope Sitam is fine."

"He broke one of his arms. I replaced it with a new one. If he had injured his head, I would have been helpless."

"How is Mantu now?"

"He was immediately taken to hospital. He remained unconscious for twelve hours. When Mantu gained his conscious he remembered nothing of his innocent phase."

"All is well that ends well."

"It was good nobody doubted. I had already left for home. So the accident was not linked to me and doubting the mannequin was out of question."

Both were laughing when they heard Aunty's bell from downstairs.

"Ice, Aunty is calling you. Go and meet her."

Ice went down stairs and found Aunty sitting on a sofa.

"What is it Aunty?"

"It is a house but not hotel where you have to eat food only. Fifteen days have passed since we have talked. Though today you are on leave still you didn't bother to come down."

"Oh, dear Aunty you don't even know how to show anger. Where do you want to go? I will accompany you."

"How do you know, I am going out?"

"Your purse is outside the Almirah. You take it out only when you have to go out."

"First you have your breakfast. We shall go and get some cloth for the curtains."

"Only on one condition."

"What?"

"You shall not stitch them at home."

"All the time I am free so what is the harm to do some work?"

"What about your backache? You are not having any sleep for the last two days."

"That…. How do you know?"

"Black Magic. I know black magic."

"Don't make fool of me. You must have seen my ointment."

"The purse and ointment talked to me. So this is black magic."

"Okay, I will get curtains stitched outside, let's get ready and move."

Ice went upstairs to get ready and saw grandpa ready to leave.

"Where are you going, now?"

"You are going to market so I thought to go and see the mannequins."

"It is fine. I shall tell you more stories at night."

" Ice, now you can call me any time you need."

Ice and Aunty went to market. Ice was so used to sell that buying was not easy for her. While they were seeing curtains she collided with a boy."

She turned around, "I am sorry."

The boy saw her, "I shall not forgive you."

Ice found the voice familiar. Looking at him she said surprisingly, "You?"

"It is me who should be surprised. What are you doing here in duty hours? Have you left the Mall or they got rid of you?"

"I am on leave."

"Your boy friend is not here?"

"My boy friend? Who?"

"The girls don't take leave without any reason."

"Wait, I will introduce you to him."

Ice called her Aunty.

"Aunty, please come here."

"What is it, have you selected something?"

"Aunty, I want you to meet Coke Mani. I used to go to his factory."

"So you are Mr. Coke. Ice always talks about you. Thanks God she has a friend to meet in this city. Otherwise her entire life is in the mall."

Coke laughingly said, "No, Aunty, she doesn't come to meet me instead she comes to see Khushi."

"Who is Khushi?"

"Ice didn't tell you…….."

Ice interrupted.

"Aunty, it is a small rabbit. He lives with Mr. Coke."

"That's very good. Let's finish with the shopping then we shall eat something."

In the meantime the boy from the shop came, "Ma'm the cloth you selected has been found, please select the colour."

"Ice, I shall see over there, you have a look here."

After Aunty left, Coke said, "Why did you tell lie without any reason?"

"If Aunty had known the truth, she wouldn't have allowed me to enter your house."

"Why?"

"Aunty has no liking for dogs. Her daughter lost her life while saving a dog. Since then she hates dogs."

"That's really sad."

"By the way what are you doing here? Have you started stitching curtains also along with clothes?"

"I am buying curtains for my house."

"House! Don't you live in your factory?"

"Factory will be at ground floor and the living room on the first."

"Nice to hear, if you need any help please do tell me."

"It is understood, you have to select the whole furniture."

"First, I have to see the house."

"When do you wish to come?"

"Let's drop Aunty on our way."

"O.K."

While talking to Coke, Ice forgot grandpa shall be waiting for her. At Coke's house Khushi welcomed her with great enthusiasm.

"How are you Khushi? You have grown up."

"Why didn't you come for so many days? I have a lot to tell you."

"What's so special?"

Coke said, "Let's go upstairs Ice. I have got the place cleaned today itself. They reached the upper portion. There were two rooms and a small hall. There was no furniture. The empty walls seemed as if they were weeping. It was an airy house.

" Nice wind is blowing and the fragrance of flowers smells great."

"There is a flower garden in the backyard, so it always smells great."

"You have got such a wonderful house, why do you live in the factory?"

"A lonely person has limited requirements and moreover work kept me occupied. Truly speaking I never had money too. Now Khushi's company is very enjoyable."

"Why didn't you give the house on rent?"

"You can see the condition of the house. First of all, it needs to be repaired moreover the stairs are from inside. Changing them will cost me a lot."

" Tell me whether you want to decorate a single room or the whole house?"

"The entire house, where I will live in with my wife and I also want a special place for Khushi."

Ice excitedly spoke, "Coke you are getting married but didn't even tell me? Let me know who is the girl?"

"You girls have the same problem. You go too far. I am talking about my future. When did I say that I am getting married right now? First of all, I have to have a decent house where she can live comfortably."

"I don't agree with you."

"Why?"

"I don't think you should marry only when you have all the comforts. If some girl is in true love with you, she will come for you not for what you are and for what you possess."

"What if I love someone so much and I want to comfort her with all the happiness possible?"

For sometime both stared at each other. Khushi was staring both of them. He stood confused.

"Why both of them are silent? Which is this language, they are communicating through eyes?"

He barked, "Ice! Coke!"

Both were startled.

"Coke, I think Khushi is hungry."

"You didn't tell me anything regarding house."

"First you get it repaired. I will take over when painting starts then we shall think of the furniture."

"By the way what shall be your charges for this job?"

Ice knew that Coke was having fun.

"You have to decide after the job is over."

They were coming downstairs while Ice heard her grandpa. He was calling her. Her attention diverted and she could not notice the broken stairs and fell down. Coke came for help but she injured her knees.

"Ice!"

"Ah!"

"How did you fall?"

"I think I was thinking something else."

Coke helped her stand but she was not able to take even a single step. Coke picked her up and seated her on chair. He brought some ice and applied it on the wound.

"It's paining even more."

"It will pain now but later you will get relief."

"No, remove it."

She tried to remove it, Coke gripped both her hands.

"Don't behave like a child."

Khushi barked, "Is it paining too much, Ice?"

Ice nodded. Again she heard grandpa calling.

"Coke, I must leave now. Aunty would have been worried."

"Take rest for a few minutes then I will drop you."

"No, I will manage."

"In such condition I won't allow you to go alone."

"Coke............."

"I don't want to listen."

After sometime they realized that they were still holding hands. Both were a bit embarrassed.

"I will get coffee for you," saying so Coke left.

Khushi came to Ice, "Why don't you heal it through magic?"

"No, we don't use magic for our benefit. Doing this will take away our magical powers."

"Let me try."

Khushi rubbed his paws over her knees, the pain was gone. As she saw Coke coming, she again covered it with ice.

"Did you remove the Ice?"

"No, not at all. I am feeling quite better now."

"I told you so."

"Thanks."

Khushi barked, It's me who should be thanked."

"Don't get upset, you can understand."

"Yes."

Ice picked him in her lap affectionately. Being happy he went away.

"Can you walk on your own or should I support you." Coke extended his hand toward Ice.

She wondered at herself when she held his hand. She stood up. Though she had no pain even then she pretended having trouble while taking steps. Coke seated her in the car. All the way back home both remained silent. Perhaps both were talking to themselves.

"I wish this journey never ends. Why am I so tensed in heart? Is it love?"

"I don't know why I feel secure in his arms? I like his company. Is it love?"

She heard Coke saying, "Ice, we are home. Should I leave you to your room?"

"No, no, if Aunty will know, she will look after me for the whole night. I will go."

"Will you be able to climb stairs?"

"I will manage, pain is also less than before."

Both said good bye to each other, Coke left. After having dinner with Aunty, Ice reached her room and found grandpa waiting for her.

"Sorry, grandpa, it took a little while with Aunty."

"Who was the boy?"

It was unexpected from her grandpa, so she got nervous.

"You must be knowing everything."

"I could have but I didn't. I wanted to listen everything from you."

"Grandpa, he is Coke. We met through business and we became good friends. He is a hard working and kind hearted person."

"Why did you go to his house today?"

"Coke wanted some advice from me to renovate his house."

"Why from you?"

"I don't know."

"Does he love you?"

"No idea."

"You love him."

"I don't know.'

"What's wrong with you, Ice?"

"I don't know."

Now, Saif was unable to hold his laugh. Watching him laugh, Ice understood everything.

"So, you were pulling my leg."

"I couldn't control my laugh otherwise......."

"You enjoy teasing me. I got scared. I am already very upset."

"You express your feeling to him, everything will be fine."

"Why should I initiate? Why not he?"

"Perhaps he is not clear."

"Let him be, I am in no hurry."

On the other hand, Coke's state of mind was even worse. Ice pouring her heart out to her grandpa but Coke had nobody. When he reached home Khushi was still awake.

"Hey, you are still awake. You didn't have your meal either. What's the reason?"

Khushi gestured towards Coke's plate.

Coke said, "I am not hungry, you have your food."

Khushi went to a corner. Coke picked him and started playing with him.

"Khushi, you too like Ice?"

Khushi barked in affirmation.

"You know Khushi, today when I touched Ice for the first time I felt on top of the world. I saw love in her eyes for me but couldn't decide whether that love was for a friend or more than that. Perhaps this is the reason that I couldn't gather enough courage to propose her. I was afraid of loosing her."

Coke kept on talking to Khushi for quite a long time, then fell asleep.

Next morning when Ice and Gunjan reached Mall, Mita told them Rahul has got the information.

Ice asked, "Which information?"

"The boy who gives you company."

"Now what will happen, Ice?"

"Nothing to worry."

Ice now was satisfied because her grandpa was back. When everybody got busy with the work, Ice had a talk with mannequins.

"How are you John and Jui?"

"We are fine since Saif has come. You have forgotten us."

"This is not possible, you all are my life."

Sitam said, "We have heard somebody else has entered in your life."

"Grandpa must have told you everything."

Jenny said, "We already knew it, we were giving you sometime so that you can understand yourself."

Attu said, "We have even designed the interior and furniture for your house."

"How did you manage to see the house?"

Ferry said, "Yesterday Saif showed us as his powers have increased considerably. His palm is like a live T.V. on which we saw everything."

"This is very nice. I shall be living in a house decorated by you."

Amber told, "Coke is a nice chap and you should not delay any further."

Before Ice could have answered, her mobile rang, she picked up the phone, "You! Why did you call?........................ I don't want to meet you."

Attu said, "You disconnected the phone? Was it Rahul?"

"Yes."

"What is the reason, you are not afraid today? He can harm Coke."

"Now grandpa is here, he will not let anything happen to my Coke."

"Okay, your Coke!"

Ice was not aware what she said. All of them teased her. Feeling shy, she absorbed herself with work. While working, she sent a message to her grandpa explaining everything. When Saif got the message, he was reading a book at Ice's room. Within no time he reached Coke's house. Coke was working on machine while Khushi was resting. Seeing a stranger he started barking.

"What happened Khushi? Why are you barking. Nobody is here."

Hearing Coke, Khushi started thinking.

Saif said to Khusi, "Only you can see me Khushi. Don't worry, I am a friend, not enemy. I am Saif, grandpa of Ice."

Khushi barked, "I wanted to meet you."

Coke said, "Khushi, keep quiet. You are disturbing me."

Saif told, "We can even talk while remaining silent. Ice must have told you."

Khushi calmed down, "Yes, I just forgot."

Saif came to him and patted him. Khushi felt very nice.

"Your touch is just like Ice's."

"You like Ice."

"Very much, I cannot see her much though Coke is also very nice."

"I want Coke and Ice to marry."

"What will happen then?"

"Then they will be living together along with you."

Khushi jumped in excitement. Coke found it very strange. "What's wrong with you Khushi? You are behaving strange. Are you alright?"

Khushi became quiet. "If I could tell Coke."

"I am here for something important, Khushi."

"Tell me."

"Coke's life is in danger, so we have to work together. If you find anything wrong you have to inform me immediately."

"How?"

"You just close your eyes, take my name and send the information. I will get it."

"And what if something happens outside the house?"

"I will take care of that. You have to inform me the moment Coke leaves the house."

"It's Tuesday today, every Tuesday Coke goes to buy raw material."

"Is it his routine?"

"Yes, and he comes late."

"Rahul can create some trouble as he must be knowing about Coke's schedule. Today, I will not leave him alone even for a minute."

Saif gathered more information from Khushi. After sometime, Coke left the house.

"Khushi, I am going out. Your meal is here. I will be eating outside."

Khushi waived his foot to say good bye. Saif seated himself on the rear seat. He kept on reading his mind which was occupied by two things, either his work or Ice.

Coke bought the needed material. While leaving, a particular cloth drew his attention. He thought Ice would look very pretty if she wears a dress of this cloth. He bought that cloth instantly. Saif kept smiling watching all this. Today after having dinner, Coke was late than usual. He thought of talking to Ice but decided not to call her, thinking she might be asleep.

Saif sent a message to Ice, "Coke wants to speak to you, Ice."

Ice dialed the number, "Hello, Coke."

"You know I was thinking of calling you."

"Then why didn't you call?"

"I thought you must be tired after a busy day and must be sleeping."

"Tell me how was your shopping today? Did you find something new?"

"Yes, today I got some fabrics that I was looking for quite a long time."

"Next time I will also accompany you."

"Will you get a leave?"

"I will manage, you need not worry."

"You sleep now. Good night."

"Good night."

Coke disconnected the phone knowingly, a jeep was blocking his car and six bad looking guys got off from the jeep. Two of them were armed with sticks. Their intentions were not looking good. Coke also got hold of his stick and came out of this car. Saif was behind him.

"Why are you people blocking my way?"

One of them said, "We have to kill you."

"Why? Have I done anything wrong. You can take whatever I have. What shall you get by killing me?"

The second one said, "Oh! He is already afraid."

Saif was watching that there was no sign of fear on Coke's face. He was holding his stick in a tight grip. He was alert. Before indulging in a fight, he wanted to know who sent them.

One of them snarled, "Why are you after Ice? Our boss will marry her."

"That girl loves me, who told you that I love her?"

"Our boss is aware of everything. Either you leave the city or you shall have to leave this world."

"Are you threatening me?"

"Our boss never threatens, he does what he says."

"If he is so brave why didn't he come himself. I think he is a coward so he had sent rented goons like you."

"We should kill the person who speaks like this for our boss."

Three goons came forward and attacked Coke. What happened next was unbelievable. Coke single handedly blasted them. Saif was astonished to see his martial arts. The rest of three were now alert as they came towards Coke. Two of them were having sticks. Coke and Saif were also focused. When Coke was fighting them one of the goons attacked at the back of his head, the blow was interrupted by Saif. He got confused as Coke had no effect of such a severe blow. On the other hand, Coke was not even aware of it. This was all with the help of Saif that the goons fled away. There was a small wound on Coke's wrist with minor bleeding there. He tied it with his handkerchief and drove his way to home.

Seeing blood on Coke's wrist Khushi barked with concern.

"Calm down Khushi, I am fine. It's just a minor wound."

Seeing Saif standing right behind Coke Khushi asked "What happened?"

"It is difficult to explain in words but your master is a brave man. Now, I will leave, you take care of him."

Khushi brought water and cloth and cleaned the wound. Coke was astonished to see his love for him.

"Khushi, you are my best friend. Now you go to sleep, I will go to a doctor tomorrow."

When Saif reached home, Ice was waiting for him.

"What happened grandpa, you are so late?"

"Some goons attacked Coke and he was injured so.............."

"Coke got injured even in your presence? You should have taken care of him."

Ice was so worried, without listening to her grandpa she called Coke. Coke was going to sleep though there was slight pain in his hand. He was surprised to see Ice calling so late.

"What is it, Ice?"

Ice spoke in a nervous tone, "Where have you been injured, Coke? Where did the goons attacked you? Why didn't you call me?"

Ice spoke nonstop while, Coke was wondering how did she knew everything.

"Why are you not replying, Coke?"

"I can talk only if you give me a chance to speak."

"Say."

"First tell me how did you came to know about the incident?"

Ice was shocked. She never considered this thing for which she became speechless. She looked at her grandpa who was relaxed and enjoying the show.

Coke repeated, "Ice, shall you answer me?"

Saif said, "Answer him."

"I am sorry."

"You tell him, you had a dream about it."

Coke was eager, "What happened, Ice?"

"I don't know. Perhaps it was a nightmare, I suddenly got up and called you. I am sorry to disturb your sleep."

"No, nothing like this. I was still awake."

" I am disconnecting now."

"Yes, I am fine. Good Night."

After the phone call Coke was thinking whether Ice really had a dream or.......................or what..........Then he thought of his stupid thinking and decided not to pay attention, and he slept.

Ice was having a tough time with her grandpa when she told, "You keep on doing such silly mistakes; soon Coke will be having doubts. I know you are concerned about Coke but you should learn to handle your emotions. You are not an ordinary girl, so your responsibilities are more."

"I shall be careful in the future, grandpa."

"Coke really fought bravely today."

"When you were with Coke, how could anyone even touch him?"

"No, Ice he never needed my help. I am happy, you choose him."

"Grandpa, please explain me further."

"Telling you shall not be that exciting, you can watch it right now."

Saif extended his hand, on his palm Ice could see the whole episode. After which Saif asked, "So, you enjoyed it?"

"Why did Coke lie to me that he was not hurt?"

"May be, he didn't want to bother you."

Ice was furious with Coke, but decided to sleep. In the morning all the Mannequins were praising Coke's bravery. Ice knew, grandpa must have shown them everything, but her mood was upset, she was quiet. She also didn't answer to any of the Mannequins.

Attu said, "Ice, if you are angry with Coke then why should we suffer?"

"I am not angry."

Ferry said, "I know you want to meet him to know his condition. Isn't it?"

"I don't know whether he had consulted a doctor as he is very careless."

"Why don't you give him a call at least?"

"No, no. I will not repeat the same mistake again or do anything that annoys grandpa."

Ice got busy with her customers. In the evening Robin called. Coke was already there. Their eyes met.

"Hello Mr.Coke."

"Ice, he is Mr.Mani."

"Oh! I see."

"Sir, why did you call me?"

"This time, Mr.Mani has come up with some sarees. I like the designs, you also have a look."

"Yes, Sir."

Ice stared the design; some of them were on paper. Ice noticed, Coke was hiding one of his hands under the table being conscious not to show it. Ice understood, he was trying to hide his wound. In the meantime, Robin's phone buzzed.

"Hello.......who...Oh! When did you come back from Africa...what? You are going back today only...Yes., I am coming."

Putting the phone, he stood up, "I have to leave right now.

Mr. Mani right now you go for ten sarees only. Ice will take care of the designs. I will take a leave now."

Robin left the place quickly. Ice took his chair as she was thinking of having some fun.

"So, Mr. Mani, your designs are not that impressive, said Ice."

Coke, who was quiet by now, laughed at this gesture of Ice.

"Mind it. I am not joking, told Ice."

"I know, tell me, how is your foot?" Coke enquired.

"It's perfectly fine; in the morning I didn't even know I was hurt."

Coke started collecting his designs.

"That is not required as both of us have same choice," said Coke.

'You forgot sometime I use to modify them."

"This is not possible here. You have to accompany me for this."

"I am on duty."

"I will pick you up in the evening."

Ice noticed, Coke covered his wrist with a saree as he was collecting the things. She pulled the saree off his wrist.

"Let me fold this saree."

Coke was caught unaware.

"Why have you tied your hand with handkerchief?"

"Nothing, isn't it looking good?"

"I don't like this at all. This green hanky doesn't go with your blue shirt. Remove it; you have tied it so tightly."

Ice got hold of Coke's hand, started to untie the handkerchief. Coke didn't say anything; neither had he courage to pull his hand back.

"What is this?"

"It's a minor wound."

"It's a deep one Coke; you were hiding it from me. Moreover you never informed me about your visit. You wanted to go back without meeting me?"

Coke was speechless.

"Why don't you say something? Answer me."

"What should I say? Whatever you said is true."

"How did you get injured?"

"Let us go to some other place as I had not taken my lunch today and I am feeling hungry."

"I don't want to go anywhere with you."

"So, you will not take me to a doctor?"

"You will not go."

"I didn't mean that."

"Don't try to fool me, let's go."

After eating they went to a doctor. Doctor dressed his wrist and advised not to move his wrist for two days. He was also advised to avoid driving. While going home, Ice drove but she was still angry at Coke who was trying to make up with her.

"Ice, you know when you get angry you look like a lizard on the wall."

Ice startled, "What? How can a face look like that?"

"A clean stainless wall."

"My face is like a wall?"

"Hey, why are you shouting? I was just praising you."

"Is this your way to praise a girl?"

"You are the first girl in my life, so you teach me how to praise."

"Why should I? Do you want to impress some other girl?"

"May be. At least I should know how."

"For this one has to look at girls but you are so occupied with your work."

"It seems you know at lot about me."

"We are home now."

"My work is also over."

"Which work?"

"To calm you down."

Ice laughed. By the time Khushi was in her lap. Ice patted him with love and got busy with her work. She didn't allow Coke to do anything. The house was in a complete mess. Ice was working at a quick pace.

"Coke, it is enough."

"Now, what I have done?"

"With such a serious injury, you worked for the whole day."

"This also, you saw in your dream?"

"No, it is obvious from your room and the mess created here."

"Initially, when I started on machine I felt pain, but once I started working I forgot my pain."

"So you decided not to see a doctor?"

"I see you have become quite sensible in my company. It's a common saying that good company pays."

"If you are through with self acclamation then will you tell me is this machine a magician? As sitting on it you lost track of everything."

"It is you, who is a magician because whenever you are with me I loose interest in everything else."

"Why so?"

"Don't you know?"

"No."

Ice who was aware of everything pretended to be ignorant. She wanted to hear it from Coke. She was eagerly looking at Coke expecting he will propose to her. Coke was short of words.

"I...............I mean, I.................I............."

"What I?"

"I also don't know."

Coke left to change his clothes without expressing his feelings. This was not what Ice was expecting. She was furious.

"Oh! God. The person who is taking so long to say I love you then God knows what's coming ahead."

Khushi said, "Why don't you say?"

"No, I want to listen from him."

"You are being stubborn."

"He should be courageous."

"He has never talked like this with a girl before."

"Even, I have not."

"How do I know?"

"You naughty."

Ice ran to give it a beating but it went to Coke for shelter.

"What happened? Isn't it enough for you to boss me around and now you are after Khushi?"

Ice didn't answer and started preparing dinner. After sometime she laid the table.

"Come on Coke and Khushi, let's have food."

"So quick!"

"How much time is required to make dinner for two?"

Khushi barked, "My food?"

"It's in your plate, go and have it."

Khushi left.

"Today I am feeling that I am at your place."

"That's good to hear, but make sure there is no machine in this house for the time being."

"Ice, today you have cooked the food but from tomorrow onwards I will have to........."

"I will be here tomorrow as well."

"What about your job?"

"I had spoken to Mr. Robin who has granted me leave."

"I cannot sit idle for two days."

"You have injured your left hand so you can make designs with your right hand."

Coke tried his best to convince Ice. He even arranged a maid who was ready to come thrice a day. Ice didn't listen anything. She took Coke's care and was back next morning.

She not only managed Coke's house for two days with maid's assistance, but gave the house a complete new look. She also took keen interest in Coke's designs. In these two days, many instances came when Coke could have expressed his feelings to Ice but he was unable to do so. Ice acted ignorant though she was aware of the things running in his mind.

They were at Doctor's clinic to get Coke's wound checked.

"Nice progress Mr. Mani. Your wound is healing quickly. Your wife has taken good care of you."

He was referring to Ice. Both of them remained silent. Coke looked at Ice who was staring at Doctor with a smile on her face. Doctor gave them some advice and they left the clinic.

"Come on Ice, I will drop you."

"It's fine."

They remained quiet on their way. Both were looking at each other without letting the other know as they didn't utter a word. Suddenly, Coke stopped the car.

"Coke! Why did you stop the car?"

"You are at home, Ice."

Ice regained his senses, "Oh! I was thinking something else."

"Was it me?"

"I have lot of better things to think about. You should take care of yourself and don't sit on the machine."

"What if I couldn't get sleep?"

"Then think about me."

"It will give me nightmares."

Ice turned back but Coke sped away with car.

Next day both of them got busy with their respective routines but the zeal for work was missing. At breakfast even Aunty asked whether she was upset but Ice remained quiet.

She didn't feel like eating and Coke prepared himself breakfast but couldn't eat it.

"Hey Ice, what you have done to me? Only two days earlier I was not even aware that what a bad cook I am."

When Ice reached the Mall, she was very calm and had no talks with mannequins. Mannequins didn't object to it as they were aware of the situation. Saif had asked them not to entertain Ice so that she can have time to prepare herself to talk with Coke. Ice was trying her best to keep herself busy in the work but her mind was not co-operating. She picked her phone to call Coke but then she disconnected it.

She thought, "Is he also thinking about me and if so he should give me a call. I should wait."

The day passed by but neither Ice called nor did Coke. After her duty was over she left for home with Gunjan in a sad mood. Suddenly, Coke appeared.

"Hello, both of you!"

"Hello!"

"What are you doing here? You should be at home and you are here?"

"Will you give me a chance to explain? I have come to take you."

"Where?"

"Just come along and see it yourself."

"Aunty will wait for me and her phone is out of order too."

"Gunjan will inform her."

"I will do. How is your hand now?"

"Both of you must go now."

Once inside car, Ice noticed Coke very happy.

"Where are we going Coke? What is the secret of your happiness?"

"We are going home and rest of the things shall be discussed there."

"Coke?"

"No questions, please. I am not going to tell anything."

Ice was thinking this must be the day, he will say it or he will stop midway. Let me read his mind but again she didn't want to do so. Let's see what happens.

Ice was welcomed by Khushi. He came to Ice with a rose in his mouth and gave it to her. He was having ribbons in its neck and feet and was looking very pretty?"

Ice complemented him. "You are looking very pretty. Is there something special tonight?"

Khushi answered, "First, you step inside."

As she entered the house, her jaws dropped in surprise. The home was decorated with candles everywhere. The twinkling candles were giving a breathtaking view. With excitement Ice looked around.

"Now tell me Coke what is so special today? Is it your birthday?"

Coke gestured her to keep silent and took out a dress from the cupboard.

"Please, wear it Ice."

"It is a wedding dress. Why did you buy this?"

"I have not purchased it, I have stitched it myself."

"So, you were busy in this for the whole day and this is why you didn't give me a single call. Whose order is this?"

"I will tell you later on, first you wear it."

Unwillingly, Ice went for the change. In the meantime, Coke also dressed himself in a smart black suit. Ice was looking amazing in her white gown. She was looking like a fairy. Seeing each other they were speechless.

Khushi, who was unaware of these silent emotions, was a mere viewer. First he pulled Ice's gown then tried same with Coke's dress but of no use. Irritated, he started barking. Both of them suddenly regained their senses.

"You are looking very beautiful."

"You have made a wonderful dress."

"It is not the dress but the person who is wearing it. Whenever you get married, you must wear this dress."

"How can I become a bride without a bridegroom?"

"Your groom is in front of you."

Ice was looking curiously at Coke who was now on his knees. He extended his hand to Ice "Will you marry me?"

Ice offered her hand with a smile. Khushi pushed a button of the music system and both danced. These were the memorable moments of their lives and they were lost in each other. Suddenly, they heard sharp gunfires. The whole atmosphere changed. They found themselves surrounded by goons with Rahul having a gun. He was firing in the air.

Ice got afraid and hid herself behind Coke.

Rahul said, "I don't care even if both of you have married, I have come to take Ice with me."

Coke and Ice were still in a bit of shock but they understood the whole situation.

Coke said, "She is not some thing, that you can take along."

"I don't know. All I know is, I love her very much and for that she has to live with me."

"Do you even know what love is? Love is to make the person happy whom you love. It doesn't mean to adopt unfair means to prove your love."

"My love is true."

"True love doesn't require guns and swords."

Rahul thoughtfully handed his gun to one of his men and asked them to leave the room.

"Now, tell me."

"Sit down Rahul, we can have a talk."

He sat down and Coke asked Ice to bring water.

"Listen Rahul! You are a nice person. You have seen Ice only once and was captured by her beauty. This is attraction but not love. Love is all about understanding each other. I also love Ice but my top priority is her happiness. If she is willing to go with you then I have no objection. So, you must control your emotions and start a new life."

Ice brought water and meanwhile she had also called her grandpa. Khushi was also ready but all of them were calm. Rahul was quiet and did not answer anything that Coke wanted him to say.

Coke continued, "I know Rahul, you have come here to kill me and take Ice along with you. But Ice loves me so she shall hate you if anything happens to me."

Rahul was weeping now, "I am sorry, all this violence is taught to me by my father. I never knew the love can be won with affection also."

With a heavy heart Rahul left the place.

Ice said, "Coke, you are wonderful. You convinced him so quickly."

"If you are honest and clear hearted then you can always convince people. My life is an open book with nothing to hide. Believing in each other strengthens our relations. Isn't it right?"

The last word of Coke moved Ice, "My life is not like yours. I have hidden a lot of things about my past."

"That is gone Ice. We have to live in present."

"What if the past is involved in the present?"

"I didn't get you."

Grandpa and Khushi stopped Ice to go further.

"Ice, he will not marry you once he knows everything."

"You will loose him."

"I know but now I don't want to hide anything from him."

"I cannot see all this."

"Me too."

Grandpa left and Khushi also went to other room. As all these talks were through mind waves, so Coke didn't hear anything.

"Why are you not saying anything Ice? You can trust me."

"I know what I am going to tell you after which perhaps you will not marry me."

"My love for you is not that weak, Ice."

Ice couldn't stop her tears. Coke was confused.

"Calm down Ice. You are worrying for nothing. I promise you......."

"No, Coke don't make any promises. I want you to accept me by heart but not for some pressure."

"Fine, if you wish so, have some water and then talk."

Ice calmed herself down with a glass of water and explained everything from her grandpa to mannequins and her magical powers. Coke was listening everything with great attention and never attempted to interfere. After telling everything Ice was quiet. Now she was waiting for Coke's response.

"You can read mind so you can easily know what I am thinking."

"I have never used my powers to get you."

Coke didn't say anything. In the Mall, the mannequins were watching live what was going on at Coke's house. All of them were eagerly waiting for Coke's response. Ice and Khushi were experiencing nervous heartbeats. Seeing Coke silent, Ice got up to change.

This was the moment when Coke spoke, "Ice! I love you."

Ice couldn't believe her ears. Khushi was dancing with two feet in air. In the Mall, all the mannequins were embracing each other. Ice's eyes were so full of tears but still Khushi made her laugh.

"Now, why tears, Ice?"

"These are out of happiness."

"It is always difficult to understand girls."

Saif made his entry and Ice ran in his arms. Coke understood.

"Grandpa, can't I see you?" asked Coke.

"Ice, go and hold Coke's hand so that he can see me," instructed grandpa.

Ice got hold of Coke's hand and immediately Coke was able to see Saif. Both of them took Saif's blessings.

"God bless you both!"

"Can anyone see you grandpa just by touching Ice?"

"No, Coke. The person should be honest and affectionate by heart."

Ice said, "Now grandpa all your worries must be over."

"Absolutely."

"Mine have increased."

"How, Coke?"

"Ice would always know about what is going on in my mind and those mannequins at the Mall too. I will not be able to have any fun."

"That's your concern."

Saif transmitted a bright light on Coke who felt a minor shock.

"What happened to me?"

"I have covered your brain and now nobody can read it, not even me."

"This sounds good, no worries now."

"Coke, you can give it a thought again as you are not going to have any dowry."

Coke knew grandpa was being sarcastic.

"I am getting you in dowry so what else I need?"

"You will take care of me?"

"Yes, as I take care of Khushi also."

"Coke! You are comparing grandpa with Khushi?"

"Let him speak Ice. In this age I have to listen such things."

Ice got angry, "Coke, you should say sorry to grandpa."

"It was he who started it."

"He is elder."

The discussions continued for a while when Coke and Saif laughed, Ice understood that they were pulling her leg. She went to change.

"You made her upset so go and make up with her."

"I was not alone grandpa, you were also having fun. Now you have to help me."

"I never forced you to join me; you started at your own will."

"What do you mean?"

"I mean, I will not go with you."

"I am not Ice. Now jokes apart and think of something to calm her down."

When Ice came out she couldn't stop laughing as she looked at both of them. Both of them were sitting on their knees with a piece of paper each with 'SORRY' written over it.

"Enough of this drama now, both of you stand up. Grandpa, we must go now as it is too late."

"I will drop you."

"There is no need of it; Ice will be at home within no time."

They said goodbye and the very next moment Ice was at her home. It was too late and Aunty was worried. She was very excited when Ice told her about her marriage. The next day all the mannequins congratulated Ice.

Amber and Ferry asked, "Hey! Ice just tell, how did Coke proposed you? Though Saif showed us but hearing from you will be different."

Ice thought, "Coke never said, I love you."

"This is not fair, Ice."

"I never thought of it."

Sitam said, "You are strange Ice as you said, you will not say I love you until he says and now you have accepted his marriage proposal."

Dish said, "Now it is of no use."

Attu said, "Why? Call him here and ask him to say in front of us."

John said, "At least you should also know the importance of our silence."

All of them said, "This is right, Ice, call him."

"Now it's my turn to have fun. Yesterday he and grandpa pulled my leg."

She dialed Coke's number.

"Yes, Madam!"

"Please come to the Mall now."

"So you are missing me a lot."

"Don't be mistaken. My friends want to meet you and if they approve you only then we can get married."

"Grandpa never told me something like this."

"Now I am telling you, so hurry up."

Before Coke could say something the line went dead.

Coke knew, Ice was having fun. With a pleasant mood he started getting ready. In fact, he also wanted to see the mannequins. Grandpa met him outside the Mall and gave him a magical ear plug to hear what the mannequins speak. Coke was welcomed by all the mannequins as he entered the Mall.

"Hello, Coke, we were keen to meet you."

"I also wanted to talk to you all."

"Tell us, what did you like so much about Ice?"

"Her stupid behavior."

"What do you like the most about her?"

"Her walk, just like a fox."

Coke didn't give any straightforward answer to the questions. Then he talked to each one of them separately. He won their hearts with his light veined wit. There was an ear plug in Coke's one ear while a mobile headphone was attached to the other ear to give the impression that he was talking on the phone.

After half an hour of conversation with mannequins Coke said, "I must leave now otherwise people will doubt."

Ferry said, "Sure you can go but not before saying 'I love you' to Ice in front of us all."

"I have no objection but Ice, first."

"I will not. You are a male so you should," told Ice.

"I have already proposed you for marriage but now it's your turn. Am I right friends?"

The mannequins were silent as they were clueless about whom they should favour.

"Why don't you say something? We called Coke here for this."

Attu said, "Look Ice, it is between both of you. So it will be better you sort out the matter without us."

Before Ice could say something Mr. Robin came, "Hello Mr. Mani, congratulations to you both. Ice, you never told me about this. Gunjan just informed me."

"Thanks, Sir. I was about to tell you."

"No problem. I am very happy. I can also take a little credit for bringing you together."

Coke said, "The whole credit goes to you, Sir. It is said that the first step is the most difficult one and it was possible only because of you."

"Smart boy. When are you getting married?"

"Next month, Sir."

"Don't forget to invite me. Though, it will make my pocket light. Ha! Ha! Ha!"

Mr. Robin went away. Later all the colleagues of Ice, congratulated them.

Coke said, "Now I must leave, I shall talk to you over phone."

Ice didn't try to stop him as it was of no use at such a crowded hour. Their lives didn't change. In day time, they remained busy with their work while Coke picked her up in the evening to spend some time together. Coke started renovation work at house. Khushi also enjoyed the evenings. Ice used to cook dinner regularly. Khushi now helped Coke without any hesitation. He used to arrange things. From Coke he also learned to operate the machine.

One day mannequins in the Mall, saw some strange persons. To clear their doubts they read their minds. They were terrorists who came to Mall with bad intentions. They wanted to seize the Mall and were conducting a survey. Knowing about their intentions the mannequins called Saif. Ice had already left with Coke. She had reduced her working hours. Saif followed them. They were staying in an expensive hotel. At night they met at one place. All of them had surveyed different places of the city and decided the biggest church of the city as the easiest target. Then they decided the date. To finalize the things, they took the unanimous decision to visit the church the next day and the meeting was adjourned.

After they left, Saif suddenly, recalled this was the same church where Coke and Ice were to get married. Should he stop the marriage? No, he cannot do this as both of them were very happy and moreover wedding cards had also been distributed. He decided not to let Coke and Ice know as they might get worried for each other's safety. He went to the Mall and talked to the mannequins.

All had different opinions but one thing was sure nobody wanted the marriage to be postponed. After much discussion, they decided, first they should be aware of the plan of terrorists, then they will make their strategy accordingly. Next day, Saif was there at Church with the terrorists. He also remained present when they met at night. They were making their plan and Saif was reading their minds. They were nine in all. They made two teams and planned to attack from two sides.

From the very next day terrorists started working in the direction of executing their plan. Though the day on which attack was to be executed was still ten days far but they had to collect ammunition. On the other hand Saif was busy making his action plan to stop them. For him it was very easy to handle them but he wanted that they should never know what had happened. He, mannequins and Khushi chalked out a wonderful plan.

The home was ready for Coke and Ice. Ice decorated it according to her taste. After having dinner, Ice was taking out her wedding dress.

"What are you doing Ice?"

"I am changing my dress."

"There are still three days left."

"I know, but now I will come here after marriage only. Aunty asked me not to meet you now."

"So you used to come here daily to meet me?"

"What do you mean?"

"I know you come here but you are always busy with cooking, decoration, Khushi and the ordinary jobs here. You hardly spend any time with me."

"Don't complain Coke, this was also necessary."

"I know but today when all the work is over you are telling me that you will not be coming again."

"Coke, I still have to do my shopping."

"Then I will come with you."

"No, Coke. Aunty has been like a mother to me and she wishes to buy things according to her liking which I cannot refuse."

"What about me? You are already having a married woman who is always busy in other domestic affairs except her husband."

Ice laughed, "Now will you drop me or I should go myself?"

Coke said nothing.

"Don't be sad Coke. Khushi is with you."

"Don't even mention his name; he remains happy only when you are here."

Khushi said, "I do all the work, Ice."

"Let me tell what he does. When you cook, he is always ready to get a command from you whereas I have to call him."

Ice stared at Khushi who took its leave quietly. On their way to Aunty's home, Coke was quiet and Ice tried to cheer him up.

Coke stopped the car, "Go, Ice."

When Coke was about to go Ice held his hand, "Will you say me goodbye like this? I want to have your cheerful and happy face in my mind for next three days, not this sad one."

"I will not be able to do that even if I try."

"What if I make you smile?"

"You are trying your best for so long."

"Let me try once more."

"As you wish."

"Close your eyes."

"Ice.........."

"Please don't say, you cannot do even this."

Coke unwillingly closed his eyes.

Ice whispered, "I love you."

Coke's eyes opened with a smile.

"Smile suits your face."

"Pink shyness on your face is less by any means."

Seeing Coke's car Aunty came out of the house, "Coke, come inside."

Both got down from the car and Coke touched Aunty's feet. Sunaina was a Hindu, so Coke respected her in this manner.

After Coke had left Aunty gave her details for the program for the next three days. Ice had taken leave from the Mall. The next day Sunaina did a lot of shopping for Ice, they had wedding songs and she performed other pious rituals like Mehndi, etc. for Ice.

When Coke called Ice, there was Mehndi on her hands, so Gunjan picked up the phone.

"Brother-in-law what is it?"

"I want to talk something important with Ice."

"Sorry, she is busy, you can talk tomorrow only."

"Hey! it is important."

Ice said, "Why you are teasing him. Give me phone."

Gunjan held the phone to Ice's ear, "What is it Coke?"

"Ice, I just wanted to know where are we going for honeymoon?"

"You are thinking of it now."

"You should have reminded me."

"I thought, you don't want to go."

"Now tell me where should we go."

"I think our home is the best place and moreover only we two are there."

"There is Khushi as well. He is like a bone in the chicken."

"Coke! He is just a child."

"This is his major problem. He never considers leaving us alone. I am even afraid of holding your hands in front of him." Ice laughed at this.

"You are laughing?"

"Sorry. I shall go wherever you like to take me."

"I will ask grandpa."

"That will be fine."

While both of them were lost in their enjoyable moments, Saif was busy in following the activities of the terrorists.

Terrorists were ready to execute their plan while Saif was preparing a magical powder. When he was packing the powder in a box he received a message from Ice.

"Grandpa, Coke wants to see you."

After completing his work, Saif went to Coke, "Yes, Coke, you wanted to meet me?"

"Grandpa, I can't decide where to go after marriage."

"You should have asked Ice."

"I asked her but she is also not sure."

"I know this is very important for you but there is something more important than this."

"I cann't get you."

Saif told him about terrorists, their wicked plan and his counter plan.

"Is Ice aware about all this?"

"No, she will be afraid as she gets worried soon about your safety."

"I was also thinking the same. Now, you tell me what can I do?"

"I have told you everything about my plan but you work according to the situation."

"Don't worry, though your plan is very interesting and our wedding is sure to make headlines."

"There is no doubt about it."

Both laughed.

As the day approached which was being awaited so eagerly, there was a great hustle-bustle in Church since morning. Coke was already there with some of his old college-mates. Mr. Robin was also there looking after the guests. All the people were there whom Ice helped sometime or the other. Many of her co-workers from the Mall were also there. Ice came with Gunjan and her Aunty. She was looking so dazzling for all the eyes were glued to her. In her white wedding gown, she was looking like a fairy. The advocate friend of Saif was also there and he offered his services as Ice's father. Ice moved further while holding his arm. It was a lovely sight.

Everybody went inside the Church. Coke took Ice's hand and they went to Father. On the other hand, the terrorists broke in from the backside along with their car. They had already planted bombs at different places and the remotes were with them. They were unaware, all the four bombs, they planted had already been neutralized by Saif. They tried to open the door of their car but it had been jammed by Saif. They had to work very hard. All the guns were in the car.

Saif received Khushi's message, "What's going on Saif?"

"Everything is fine here, is the marriage over?"

"Hardly ten more minutes."

"I will keep them busy."

"Will you not see this wonderful event?"

"I can see all that any time."

"Oh! I just forgot, your brain functions same as a satellite."

Coke and Ice accepted each other as husband and wife in front of Father amidst thunderous clapping. Everybody welcomed the lovely couple.

Outside, Saif opened the dickey and the terrorist's quickly picking their guns left for their respective positions as per the plan. Saif sprinkled on them the magical powder. Three of them approached the main door to block it but before they could start firing their bodies started itching. Guards were on a run when they saw them. They closed the door with great difficulty and started firing in the air.

Everybody in the hall was shocked.

One of them said, "I think something has gone wrong outside."

"We should go and have a look."

Ice whispered to Coke, "What is it?"

"Nothing, grandpa has arranged something special, let's see."

Ice couldn't understand what he was saying but she came out along with others. What they saw outside was completely unbelievable. All the three terrorists were crazily itching. They were falling again and again. They tried to pick their guns but their hands seemed to have glued to their itching bodies. They started crying.

Robin asked, "What is going on Coke?"

"I don't know, Sir. They seems to be terrorists."

The advocate laughed, "I have never seen such terrorists through out my life. I think they are a bunch of jokers."

"We should check their guns whether these are real or fake one."

Khushi got hold of a gun. Robin and the advocate surveyed the guns.

"These are real guns."

"They have planned to make us hostages."

"But right now they are doing something else."

Father called for everybody's attention, while the terrorists had started to get rid of their clothes, Coke heard Saif's voice.

"Coke, there are nine of them. You assemble them at one place until the police comes."

Coke said to the advocate, "Uncle, we should inform the police."

He was laughing. "I shall do that."

"I shall see if there are more of them."

Coke and his friends assembled them. They were in a poor state and continuous itching were making them dance. All of them were left with a single cloth on their bodies. All the guests were laughing madly.

Aunty asked, "Ice, what are they doing?"

Ice asked Coke while laughing, "I think you knew it."

"Grandpa told me the previous night."

"Stop this now."

"Let it goes on, it's so hilarious."

After sometime, they became unconscious. The police arrived.

"How did you people managed to control them?"

Advocate said, "We shall give you details afterwards, first you take them away."

Advocate happened to be a known figure of the town, so all the proceedings were over within no time. But soon the Media and News channels appeared on the scene. Many people had recorded whole event. Soon, the news spread like fire all over the country and lakhs of people saw 'Coke weds Ice' on all the news channels.

In the night Sunaina gave an elegant party. When Sunaina presented Ice in a red bridal dress Coke was stunned. On stage, both looked very pretty. Everyone congratulated them but the morning couldn't have been better.

Gunjan said, "You know Ice, your wedding is the talk of the nation."

Robin said, "I am going to remember it my entire life."

"God's immense blessings are on you."

The marriage was accomplished in a joyful manner. Coke and Ice were talking in their room.

"Hey! Ice, I think you are tired."

"To some extent, but among all this we forgot a very important thing."

"What is it?"

"We didn't meet grandpa and took his blessings."

"I don't know about you but I met him twice."

"You should have told me."

"How could I, we were never alone."

"You are right. It is my mistake. The media people made me crazy."

After being silent for a while, she said, "You knew everything. Why didn't you stop grandpa?"

In the meanwhile Saif came, "Why are you shouting at him, Ice? He had no idea about this. It was me who wanted to make your wedding somewhat special."

"What is the use of all this?"

"It makes a lot of sense."

"How?"

"Your wedding dress got lot of appreciation and perhaps you don't remember that one of the media person told you, the dress was made by Coke. Coke is going to get good business. Now, tell me how do you like my wedding gift?"

"Oh! Grandpa, you are a super hero and I........"

"You can never forget me which I know this pretty well."

Coke said, "Your presence is the most precious gift for us."

"I know Coke. It's too late so both of you take some rest. We shall leave now. Let's go Khushi."

"No, I will sleep here only."

Coke and Ice were surprised. Saif handled the situation.

"Ice has got a place for you down stairs."

"I will guard Ice."

"Coke is there."

"He is a sound sleeper and can't look after her."

Saif couldn't find the words to convince it. He helplessly looked at Coke and Ice and left. Coke made gesture towards Ice.

Ice said "Khushi, I have to talk to Coke."

"Then I am sitting outside; call me when it's over."

Khushi left and sat beside the gate. Coke gestured Ice to close the door. Ice refused to do so. Coke peeped and saw Khushi looking towards the door. Then Coke saw Khushi's ball. He threw it downstairs and Khushi ran behind the ball. As Khushi ran after the ball, Coke closed the door.

Ice laughed and got up.

"Now where are you going?"

"I have to change."

"And if I want to see you in these clothes."

Ice said nothing.

"You are looking beautiful."

Coke was now very close to her.

"Ice, you know we are married but................"

"What?"

"I still don't feel it."

"How you are going to feel it?"

"I will show you."

Coke switched off the lights. Khushi was barking outside.

In the morning, Ice prepared tea and called Coke.

"What is it?"

"Get up, tea is ready, you also have to get ready."

Coke opened his eyes and while having tea he saw Ice doing packing. "Why are you packing my clothes?"

"We have to leave the house in two hours."

"Where are we going?"

"Honeymoon."

"Where?"

"I am not going to tell you."

"I doubt your plans."

"There is no time to joke around, be quick and give me a hand."

"Yes, madam."

Coke didn't make queries. They left Khushi in care of grandpa and headed towards airport. As they were getting seated the plane, Coke said, "So, we are going to Singapore."

"Yes."

"This time of the year, booking for Singapore would have been difficult."

"Mr. Coke you are going with me. There shall be no problem."

"So you have already planned whole thing without telling me."

"I wanted to gift it as a wedding gift to you."

"I didn't give you anything."

"You have given me the most beautiful gift even before marriage which I will keep close to my heart forever."

"What is it?"

"My wedding dress. You know Coke, that is the most expensive dress for me in the whole world."

"Thanks."

"Coke, when I saw you first I never knew that........"

"...............that you will love me."

"Yes, you thought of it?"

"Not to this extent, but I liked your pretty looks."

"Tell me what else do you like about me?"

"So you are in a mood to listen some compliments?"

"You can say that."

Lost in these talks, they reached Singapore. Time they spent there was immemorable. Coke had strictly instructed Ice not to use her powers as he wanted to enjoy honeymoon like a normal human being. Ice was habituated reading others thoughts but she couldn't disobey Coke. One night as they were roaming on the streets of Singapore four goons surrounded them.

"Don't move, you both."

Ice asked, "Still, I don't have to use my powers?"

"No."

Coke asked them, "What do you want from us? We have nothing."

"Your girl friend is very pretty. We are taking her with us."

Coke turned furious, "What do you mean?"

"Don't worry; she will be with you in the morning."

All of them laughed loudly. Before they could think of anything Coke gave them a severe beating. Ice was also confused.

"It was even quicker than my magic."

They all were in a bad shape but Coke was still beating them.

"Calm down, Coke, let's leave this place."

"No, Ice, I will get them arrested so they don't dare to tease any good people in the future."

Coke got full cooperation from Singapore police. While returning after their ten days stay both were very happy. Especially, Ice was in high spirits.

"Why are you so quiet Coke? I am doing all the talking."

"That is what I was thinking of. You were not so happy even when we came here."

"I will meet everybody — grandpa, Khushi and my dear friends at the Mall. If I had the chance, I would have taken all of them with me."

Coke was silent.

"I think you don't like going back?"

"Once we are back your attention will be diverted. There are many distractions like mannequins in the Mall, grandpa at home and Khushi in our room. We are not going to enjoy any intimate moments."

"Nothing of this sort will happen Coke. Initially, I never knew what you expect from me but now as a wife I know my duties. I shall give you no chance to complain."

Coke was smiling. Ice was happy to meet grandpa and Khushi. She made them see all the stuff they recorded during their trip. Khushi was giving full attention to them but Saif was thinking something seriously. Khushi helped Ice with cooking and Coke got busy with grandpa. He could see sadness on Saif's face but didn't say anything. After dinner everybody took leave to their respective places. Ice was also getting ready to sleep. She was surprised to see Coke going downstairs in his sleepers, "Where are you going at this late hour?"

"I am not sleepy so I am thinking of make some designs."

"You were blaming me on the plane now see who is getting busy."

"I will not go if you don't want me to; I will do whatever you say."

Ice understood what Coke was suggesting, "It will be better if you go down."

"I was thinking to stay back."

"I am feeling sleepy, Good night."

Ice covered herself with a sheet and Coke went out laughing.

"That's good for Ice had no doubt."

He quickly went to Saif.

"What is it Coke? You are still awake! Is there some problem?"

"Yes, there is a problem which I would like to know from you."

Saif didn't answer his question.

"You can trust me."

"You don't need to tell me. I, myself wanted to tell you but Ice is so happy for which I didn't had the courage to tell."

"What is so serious?"

"The Mall is getting sold."

Coke was shocked, "What do you mean?"

"The Mall and mannequins are in danger."

"How shall Ice bear all this? Those mannequins are her life."

"I know we have to find some way to stop it from getting sold."

"How is it possible? Anyone can sell his or her possession."

"You are right but it is possible only if property is in one's possession."

"I didn't understand."

"The land on which the Mall is situated belongs to me. I am the real owner and if somebody is the next heir it is Ice."

Coke was still confused. Saif told him all the details.

Coke asked, "Do you have a plan?"

"I am not getting to any conclusion."

"I think you should ask your advocate friend for help."

"You mean Manas. That's a good idea but you will not be able to answer most of his questions and without satisfactory answers he won't take the case in his hands."

"You have to come in the picture."

"Coke, you don't know Manas. He doesn't believe anything before or after death. I have to even prove my identity."

"We shall do it grandpa. As we are fighting for a noble cause God's blessings shall be with us."

"You meet him tomorrow but tell nothing to Ice."

"This will not be right. Ice will be with us in this fight. She is my strength so don't make her my weakness. She is brave and knows how to act in a particular situation."

Suddenly, Ice's presence startled everybody.

"You are still awake?"

"I thought you must be working so I came to company you. But here I am being discussed so I must know the reason."

"I have already told everything to Coke so it will be better if you ask him."

Ice looked at Coke and he said, "Let's go to sleep Ice as tomorrow you have to go to the Mall."

While entering the room Ice said, "You are changing the topic."

"It was you who changed the topic in front of grandpa."

"What did I do?"

"Why don't you say, you were not able to sleep without me?"

"I have not shameless like you. Now you tell me…."

Coke placed his finger on her lips.

No questions, we will talk tomorrow.

Coke went to sleep while Ice kept glancing at him and then she too slept. On the other hand, Coke who was still awake was thinking that if he tells her the whole story, she will not be able to sleep.

In the morning, while having breakfast in the presence of grandpa Coke asked, "Ice you must be having advocate uncle's card. Please give it to me."

"Why? What's the emergency?"

"Grandpa wants him to plead our case."

"Which case?"

"Oh! God. Don't you know? The land on which the Mall is constructed is owned by grandpa and you are the real owner now. Grandpa wants to transfer that land in your name."

"I don't want to do all this. Whatever we have got is sufficient. Greed is not good for humans. We shall lead a peaceful life. I don't want to come into the lime light."

"It is grandpa's wish."

"Please, grandpa, I need nothing."

Saif quietly and helplessly looked at Coke. As both of them were staring at each other Ice smelled something wrong.

"Both of you are hiding something from me. Tell me the truth."

Saif said, "We have to tell the truth."

"You tell her, I will join you shortly."

Coke quickly left the place. After sometime his car was in front of an impressive Bungalow. The watchman asked his name and reason behind his visit and the gate was opened for his car. He was sitting in a hall like room. After sometime Mr. Manas Rai came.

"Namaste, Sir."

"Hello, dear. Sorry to keep you waiting."

"No, I am well aware of your busy schedule and shouldn't have come without an appointment."

"We should not waste time in meaningless talks. Let's come to the point."

"You know the land of the Mall was in the name of Ice's grandpa which was taken forcefully. We have come to know that those people are selling it. Before they sell the Mall, we want to put our claim in the court."

"Have you got all the required documents?"

"We have all the records."

"Show them to me, only then we shall take the next step. Tomorrow evening I can spare some time."

"It will be a great pleasure if you visit us. There are certain things we want to show you but it's not possible to bring them here and it shall be of great help while filing the case."

Manas kept on staring at him for a while and said, "O.K., as you wish. I shall bring the documents there."

When Coke was about to leave, Manas said, "You can pick me up at six in the evening."

"Thank you, Sir."

"One thing, I like to be on time."

"I know this."

On the other hand, Ice had already known everything. When she reached the Mall, she was somewhat saddened but when she met the mannequins she got cheered up. Mannequins also knew the reality. They were confident that Saif and Ice will save the Mall. Everybody welcomed Ice.

"Hello! Ice, How are you?"

"How was your journey?"

"Did Coke take good care of you?"

"We came to know some dangerous people attacked you."

"Hey! Ice, why don't you say something?"

"Has Coke told you to not to talk to us?"

"For God's sake, please be quiet. You are not giving me a single opportunity to speak even and moreover you are firing nonstop questions and now you have blamed Coke as well. He is so worried about you people."

All the mannequins laughed and Ice understood, they were pulling her leg.

Ice didn't have much chance to talk to them as the employees of the Mall surrounded her. Everyone congratulated her. After sometime, the customers started pouring in and everybody got busy in their respective duties. Then Ice again started to talk with the mannequins.

"Ice, do you think, Coke has suggested the right way?"

Amber said, "I don't think that we shall be able to get this land back through justice."

Ferry said, "We should answer the wicked people in their own language."

Sitam said, "Did you get a call from Coke?"

Ice said, "He said, after meeting the advocate uncle he shall be coming here."

Dish called, "Ice, Coke is looking for you."

"Where is he?"

"He is talking to Jui."

Ice went there quickly and saw Gunjan and Coke having a talk. Coke was adjusting Jui's hair.

Gunjan said, "It is very strange Coke, you also love these lifeless mannequins exactly as Ice does."

"Yes, I like them very much and if I get the permission I will take them home."

Ice came and said, "What happened Coke? Is your work over?"

"Yes, he has agreed. I will go to pick him up in the evening. Returning from market first I will pick you up and then together we shall go to his place."

"That will be fine."

"Carry on with your work, I will meet everybody and then go."

Ice got his point and went away smilingly. Coke met each and every mannequin and answered their questions.

Sitam said, "I don't think Coke, it will be so easy."

"There is no harm in at least giving it a try."

"This will only be the wastage of time and moreover we have powers with us."

"I know this but success achieved on the basis of your own courage tastes different. Magic should be used to increase power and not to make ourselves weak."

In the end, all agreed to Coke. In fact, all of them had deep faith in Coke and wanted to see him winning. When Coke left all the mannequins praised Coke and Ice was very proud of his.

In the evening when Ice and Coke came home with Manas Rai, Khushi opened the door.

Manas Rai was surprised, "Who opened the door?"

"Uncle, see here, it's Khushi who opened the door."

"He is so small; can he look after the house?"

"Sir, don't be mistaken by his size, he is very wise."

"I know small people are quite wise. You can take me as example."

He laughed loudly. Coke showed him all the relevant papers. He reviewed them for a long time. After which Ice gave him some details regarding her past. But there was no mention of Saif and his magic. At the dinner table Manas was quite impressed by the menu as all the dishes were his favorite ones. As he was eating quietly, Ice offered him a square parantha (pancake) of carrots. Manas was stunned and tears rolled down his eyes as he started eating it. He remembered that such paranthas only Saif used to make for him. The taste was also the same.

Seeing Manas's state of mind Ice asked, "What happened Uncle? Didn't you like the prantha?"

Manas said in a serious tone, "Where is Saif?"

Ice and Coke looked at each other but they were speechless.

"I want to meet Saif right now."

"What are you saying, Uncle, you know that grandpa is……."

"I don't want to listen. You can fool the whole world but not me. Nobody can cook a *parantha* like this except him."

The voice of Manas now raised. Then Saif's said, "Hey! You dwarf, why are you shouting like this?"

Manas looked all around, "Saif! Where are you? Let me see you. You are with me after such a long time and still you are hiding of me. If you were alive why don't you come before me?"

"I would have only if I was alive."

"Then…. is it your spirit?"

"I know that you don't believe all this stuff and that's why I never came to you. Even today, I would have not, if Ice didn't need you."

"You think I am so low that I would not trust my friend?"

Manas started weeping then he felt Saif's hand on his shoulder.

"Is this you?"

"Yes."

"So, I can touch you."

"Yes."

"Can we embrace each other?"

The next scene was quite emotional. Both the friends were weeping in each others arms. Ice, Coke and Khushi were also weeping. For some time they forgot others around of them. Later Saif offered food to Manas recalling their school days. Ice and Coke were able to understand a few things but most of the things going on were beyond their understanding. They kept silent. Coke said to Ice, "Can you believe, he is a top shot lawyer of the city?"

"This is for the first time I am looking grandpa with him."

"Uncle wanted to go back soon."

"Do you think he will go now?"

Coke thought to have some fun, "Excuse me, Sir, you had to go somewhere as you are very punctual of time."

Manas had a loud laugh, "Thanks for the reminder, Coke."

He picked up his phone and issued some important instructions and both the friends were lost again.

"Ice, I think their talks are endless, so why should we spoil our night."

Ice pushed his hand away and said, "You should not be so shameless. They are our guests, if they need something?"

"Grandpa is with him."

"If you want to sleep then you can go, I will stay here."

"It is not fair."

"Coke, sometimes you behave like a child."

"If I want to spend sometime with my wife what's wrong in it?"

"Wife has lot of other things to take care of during the day other than her husband."

"But nights belong to both of them."

"We are having useless discussion."

In the meantime Manas called.

"Come here kids."

"Yes, Uncle."

"From now on, no uncle or Sir likes talks. You can call me your younger grandpa. Is it fine?"

"Yes, Sir. I mean grandpa."

"Now both of you go and sleep. We shall start working tomorrow."

"If you need something?"

"Saif is with me. I am with him since I was a child and we have grown young together. I never knew I would be dwarf after having food prepared by him."

He had a good laugh and was joined by everybody.

While laughing Manas said, "Ice, you need not to worry about this case. I and Saif will handle it and shall take your help only when required."

"You can wake me when you want to go."

"No need of it. I will drop this pigmy."

"Hey! At least don't embarrass me in front of kids."

"Why? Do you look very tall to them?"

The leg pulling continued. Ice and Coke went off their room.

"Coke, why didn't you tell me in the night?"

"You won't be able to sleep for the whole night which I never wanted."

"Thanks, for being so caring."

"No, you are getting it wrong. See, if you don't sleep, you wouldn't allow me to sleep either and I am quite sleepy."

Ice threw a pillow at him, "You are never serious."

"Will you like it if I change myself?"

"Who told you this?"

"Your eyes. If you can read mind, I can read eyes."

Ice's sweet laughter melted in the atmosphere. Downstairs, the talks between Saif and Manas had shifted to serious discussion.

"You know Saif, this case is not very easy."

"I know, but we two can handle it easily. You must be remembering the poor farmer whose land was handed over to him without any proof."

"Those were illiterate people and got afraid of magic but this time the opposition is strong and deceitful."

"Don't worry. I am confident. Your brain and my powers will do wonders."

"Amen."

Saif and Manas chalked out further plan. In the morning, when Ice came down both of them were no where to be seen. There were two cups of tea on the table. Ice knew, they had a long discussion overnight. At the Mall, mannequins complained to Ice.

"Ice, why didn't Saif showed up yesterday?"

"I think they were talking till morning."

"Who are you talking about? We know that Saif is quite upset for us."

"Now, nothing to worry about. We have found a way out."

All the mannequins lit up then Ice told them everything. Later she got busy with her work. Time kept on passing. Saif was very busy as well as happy. Coke was having good orders but he was never greedy for more. Ice and Coke managed to spend time together. Fifteen days later Manas informed that he had filed the suit and the case will come up for hearing in a short time. Ice and Coke were happy to know this.

Manas and Saif were aware, now they will have to be extra careful for Coke and Ice. Today they were discussing this topic only.

"Tomorrow when those people will come to know, the land worth crores of rupees is going to be slipped off their hands."

"Do you think they will sit quietly?"

"Legally, they cannot do any harm."

"Such people are not abided by law."

"You are right Saif. We should make some arrangement for the safety of the kids."

"Coke's maximum time is spent at home and moreover he is quite capable of defending himself. Ice spends her maximum hours outside and travels alone."

"Being a girl she will be a soft target for them and she is the real owner too. You have to be with her round the clock."

"I know my duty."

Saif did not tell Manas, about the powers of the mannequins.

If he would have done so even then Manas wouldn't have believed. Saif talked to mannequins in the night.

"You have to carefully scan every visitor over here."

"We will do whatever you say."

Dish said, "Still, I think Ice is in great danger."

Attu said, "If there is any danger we can only inform Saif but can't do anything."

"You are not helpless as you have assumed. On many occasions you have helped Ice out of trouble."

Sitam said, "That is limited inside the Mall but not outside."

Ferry said, "This time more risk is involved outside."

Saif said, "Whoever wants to harm Ice, is sure to come to the Mall once or twice after which I will take charge."

All the mannequins were quiet.

Saif said, "I know it is a hard duty, after all reading mind of so many people is a tiresome job."

"You don't worry. We will try our best and identify the person at the earliest."

From the very next day, mannequins took charge of their duty. Now they were more focused on the other people than Ice. Till evening Attu was in a bad shape. Since he was placed near the bathroom and whenever a person went inside, he was thinking of his upset stomach. Fed up Attu called for Ice.

"Change my place right now."

"What happened?"

"Every person going in and out from here thinks to relief himself from the nature's call."

"It is your mistake to read the minds of these people."

"I don't feel any pleasure in doing so. Saif has asked me to do so."

"Why?"

Now it suddenly striked Attu which he is not supposed to disclose to Ice. What should he do now?

"I don't know Ice."

"So you are not going to tell me."

"I am telling the truth."

"Why your face has turned pale?"

"You are making a fool of me. We cannot change the colour of our faces."

Ferry teased from a distance, "There is no need to make a fool out of him as he is already………"

Both started to have verbal exchange. In the meantime, Mita took Ice with her.

Ferry said, "Ice has gone now, be quiet."

Attu said, "So you were talking like this so that Ice can listen, but why?"

"What should I do with you Attu? First of all you were about to disclose her everything and when I tried to distract her attention…."

"I got it Ferry. I'm really an idiot. Thanks for the help."

" Get back to work."

Attu again started with the same routine which he hated doing. Then he read the mind of a passerby, "I shall not spare her, what she thinks of herself, I will not let my wealth worth million, sink even if I have to kill her."

Attu without thinking sent message to all the mannequins, "A person wants to kill Ice. He is wearing black pants and flowered shirt."

All the mannequins started to keep an eye over him. He started to search for a girl whose name he didn't know. Mannequins have also called for Saif. Ice was ignorant about all this.

"Tell me if I can help you in any way."

"No thanks."

"I think you are looking for something. You can tell me."

He looked here and there and took out a picture from his pocket, "I'm looking for this girl. Do you know her?"

Ice looked at the picture, "She is Shaina. She used to work here but now she has left job from here."

"Why? Did she hit some treasure?"

"Yes, she did. She didn't go for it."

"I can't get you."

"First of all, you tell me why are you interested in this girl?"

"She lured my son to her love and now he doesn't think about anyone else except her."

"She is not at fault rather your son trapped her in his lies."

"What lies?"

"Shaina never liked rich boys. So, Monty used to come here in simple clothes riding on a bicycle. When Shaina came to know about truth, she permanently left this place."

"Now, Monty is looking for her and is always lost in thoughts. Can you arrange a meeting with Shaina for me?"

"What is the use of it? She is already gone from your son's life. Now, what do you want?"

"I've made a mistake. I was thinking of getting her killed without knowing the truth. I will marry my son to her."

"You are serious?"

"Honestly."

Ice asked mannequins' opinion and all replied in affirmative.

Seeing Ice quiet, he said, "What should I do to make you believe?"

"You don't need to do this. I don't know about the

whereabouts of Shaina though I can tell you her parent's address. You can meet them."

The person left the place satisfied. Ice also got busy with her work. Attu was now in a problem as he without knowing the whole thing alarmed everybody and called Saif as well.

John said, "You and your childish habits!"

Jenny said, "You should have understood the whole situation first."

August said, "So many years have passed and we can have an idea of a person by his or her looks."

Everybody was scolding him. Saif came to his rescue.

"Don't scold him. We should be happy that somebody is going to start a new life. Attu, I'm not angry with you. You continue with your good work and can call me anytime."

"Thanks, Saif. From now on, I will talk to you directly."

Saif left the Mall. A week passed by. Every time mannequins had doubt they analyzed the whole situation and on every occasion it happened to be something else. One day Saif informed mannequins, after fifteen days there will be the first hearing of the case in the court.

"We have to be extra careful for these fifteen days. Those people will like to see the case closed even before it begins."

Sitam asked, "Why so?"

"They know entire documents they possess, are forged. Everybody knows that Manas doesn't take a false case in his hands and so far he has not lost even a single case."

After two days a man rushed into the Mall. Dish had no idea of this man. He straightaway dashed to Ice.

"You are Ice?"

"Yes."

"I have come to see you."

"Anything specific?"

"I want to purchase furniture for my house and want you to help me."

"That's fine, Sir. If you purchase all the furniture from here then we shall surely help you."

"I'll purchase from here only but first you will have to see my house."

"That's not needed. I don't visit anybody's house. We shall ask you a few questions related to your house. Be assured about the job it will be to your liking."

During all this discussion Dish and Ferry were trying to get an idea about what is going through that person's mind.

"It seems quiet difficult to take this girl with me. I don't know why boss ordered to bring her in a respectable manner. It would have been better if he had asked to shoot her right here."

All the information was transmitted to Saif. Now there was no doubt left. Ice made an excuse to call next day. Saif accompanied that person. The man went to an old but elegant house. Neither he was stopped nor he talked to anybody. He took the stairs and went to a room in the corner.

"Come, Chunky. Is the job done?"

"Not yet but it will be done."

"When?"

"It will be over by tomorrow evening. It is quite difficult to act nice. I was even afraid to talk over there. Boss, please don't assign me such jobs in the future."

"Sometimes, you have to be nice."

"Can I be off or you want something else to me do?"

"No, you enjoy yourself but be sure to complete the job by tomorrow. This kidnapping is worth rupees one crore."

After hearing all the conversation Saif left the house. Everything was clear to him. At night he held a meeting with the mannequins for further course of action.

"How are we going to plan further?"

Dish said, "We should inform Ice about this."

Sitam said, "Then we have to tell her the whole story."

Attu said, "Saif, you can refuse her to go with that person."

"What may be the reason behind this?"

Everybody was applying his or her mind.

Suddenly Sitam said, "What, if he isn't able to come to the Mall?"

Attu said, "If he wants to come here then he will be here."

"That is not necessary. Anything can happen on the way."

Attu said, "You talk rubbish. How can something happen to him, if we think so sitting here?"

Attu was confused but all the mannequins and Saif got the idea. They planned how to stop him on the way to the Mall. In the morning, Coke noticed that Saif was seen nowhere. He asked Ice.

"Where has grandpa gone so early in the morning?"

"He would have gone somewhere. He also didn't come the whole night."

"You didn't ask?"

"Coke, you are well aware that none can harm grandpa. Then why should I worry for him? Moreover I am very busy today."

Ice was really busy in her work and Khushi was helping her. Coke was on the machine but his attention was somewhere else. He was thinking, 'I am sure grandpa has got some clue. Perhaps I could have helped him.'

Saif was in Chunky's car to fail its brakes. He had not much knowledge about the parts of car so he was asking Manas.

"Hey! Manas what are you doing?"

Manas was surprised, "When did you come here? Get out, I am not wearing any clothes."

"So you are in the bathroom."

"You can't see that?"

"I am not there; I am just transmitting my voice to you."

"Thank God. I was scared. By the way where are you?"

"I want to put a fault in the car of a bully, you tell me how to do it."

"How can I tell you like this? You will not understand."

"You just think in your mind, how to do, I will get it."

After some hard work Saif succeeded. Chunky came out and eased himself in another car and fled away. Saif cursed himself.

"What happened Saif? Has he started the car?"

"Yes, but it was a different one."

"You should have an idea which car he will take."

"Leave it. Now, let's try our luck with this car."

"It will be difficult to put some fault in the running car. You try to do something with his brain."

Saif was not sure of what to do. He was thinking, what can he do to his brain. Suddenly a thought flashed in his mind and he erased the meeting of Chunky with Ice from his brain.

Chunky was thinking, "I have promised the boss of bring the girl but what should I do if she refuses? I should have met her first. Though I went to the Mall yesterday then why didn't I meet her? Sometimes my mind......."

Saif reached the Mall and told the whole story to Ice. Ice was very disappointed, "You should have told me earlier as well. All the time you keep on bearing all the tensions."

Dish stopped her, "This is not the right time to argue,

Chunky will be here any moment. We have to think of doing something quickly."

Ice was thinking that there was not enough time left to call Coke. Suddenly a smile appeared on her face. Before anybody could know the secret of her smile Chunky was in front of her. Since he was unaware of the previous meeting, he narrated a different story to Ice, "I want some furniture for my office. I will be grateful if you spare some time to visit my office."

Ice was struggling to control her laugh. Yesterday it was his house, today it is office and God knows what is going to be tomorrow. I have to tight his screws.

Ice said, "I have to go to the bank for ten minutes. After which I shall accompany you."

"You come with me. You can do your work on the way."

"I don't want to bother you. You just give me your address and I will be there."

As expected, he took her to the bank. Chunky kept waiting in the car and Ice entered the bank. On her way, she told Saif about her plan. As Ice reached to bank, Saif reached Chunky's boss. He was busy watching T.V. The bids on some match were in progress. Saif quietly picked up his mobile and dialed Chunky's number.

"Hello boss, I shall be coming shortly."

Saif said in his boss' tone, "Here something gone wrong, you leave the girl and reach here now."

"What about the girl?"

"Don't you understand what I am saying? Leave her and come back fast."

Saif disconnected the line. Chunky was very confused but could not ignore the boss, so he fled away from the sight. Saif and Ice were relieved seeing him leaving.

"Thank God, he had no doubt."

"There was no question of any doubt as your plan was excellent."

"But don't repeat the same mistake in near future."

"Never. Now you go to the Mall. I shall go and see what Chunky gets from his boss."

"I also want to see."

"I will show you in the night."

Ice returned to the Mall smiling and Saif already reached the room where Chunky was suppose to face his boss.

Chunky came in a hurry, "What happened boss? Why did you call me back? I was about to bring the girl."

The boss was stunned, "What do you mean, you were about to bring the girl? Where is she?"

"It was you who called me back. You spoiled all the hard work done by me."

Boss got hold of Chunky's collar, "I will empty my gun in your brain. The work given to you is still not done and moreover you are blaming me for all this?"

Both of them kept fighting and arguing for quite a long time. When Chunky showed him the mobile number, boss was stunned. After seeing his call in Chunky's phone he had to admit that Chunky was not wrong. "I am totally confused. Nobody dares to enter this place."

"Calm down Boss. I think someone amongst us, is working for them."

"I will smash his brain out. Tell me his name."

"This is something you have to think, Boss. Who else was here at that time?"

Now their talks were boring for Saif but he had to stay there. He had to know about their future plans. Saif was aware that these people were really dangerous. They could go to any extent to accomplish the job at hand. Boss had a full army of goons with latest ammunition. They decided that Chunky will go to Ice once more. On the other hand Saif, Ice and Coke decided that Ice will ask him to come next day so that they could have some extra time. Saif taught some magic tricks to Ice so that she could defend herself.

Next day when Chunky came to Ice, she pretended to be angry with him. She complained a lot to him. Chunky was not used to such scolding. He controlled himself with great difficulty. Ice was enjoying his state of mind. She asked him to come the next day and promised to accompany him. Talking to himself he left the place. While Ice was smiling mannequins were quite worried.

Jenny said, "Ice you teased him for quite a long time."

Ferry said, "You know what was going in his mind?"

August said, "His hand had twice reached his gun."

Everybody was speaking in tandem.

Ice was fed up, "Stop all this. I knew everything but I was aware that he can do no harm to me."

Dish told, "Ice, we are concerned about you and not him."

"I know that dear but there is no fun in getting afraid. You tell me, didn't you enjoy what he was going through?"

All nodded in affirmation. In the evening when Coke came to take Ice, she said, "You never told me that you were coming to pick me up."

"Grandpa has sent me. We have prepared an excellent plan."

"What is it?"

"Let's go, I will tell you on the way."

"There is still an hour left to go home."

"I have spoken to Mr. Robin."

On their way, Coke told Ice that grandpa has decided to camp in a jungle for seven days.

"What shall we do there?"

"You will learn magic from grandpa while I and Khushi will do some mountain caring."

"So, Khushi is also going with us, it will be a great fun."

" It is Khushi who matters, I am nowhere in the picture?"

"So, you want me to compliment you?"

"I will not mind if you do so."

"For the time being, you have done nothing that needs attention. Besides, I also don't believe you these days."

"Please don't believe me for some time?"

"What do you mean?"

"I mean, we are going to a jungle and in the jungle a person has to live as a savage."

Among these talks they reached home. Ice saw, packing was almost over. Khushi was very excited as it was his first outing.

"Grandpa, you managed all the packing by yourself?"

"Coke and Khushi helped me. Now you pack your clothes so that we can leave."

"If we leave now, it will be dark when we reach there. How shall we arrange the camp in the dark?"

"You just get ready, leave the rest to me."

After an hour they were on the road leading to jungle. Once they entered the jungle, Saif took charge of driving from Coke. It was not possible for Coke to drive in the dense forest. Saif knew the jungle very well. After half an hour they reached a plane area surrounded by hills. Two camps were already there. Saif lit a lamp in the camp.

"Grandpa you did all this?"

"I came here to meditate. These stone benches are also created by me. You can arrange your bedding on them. It is already late. You should sleep now. I shall show you lot of things in the morning."

Saif and Khushi went to the other camp to sleep. Coke brought the things needed while Ice arranged the bed. Coke switched on the tape. The sweet music made the atmosphere romantic. Ice turned around to see Coke inviting her to dance.

"Coke, it is already late night."

"There is no hurry to wake up early."

Ice couldn't refuse Coke. Though she was quite tired but she enjoyed the moments with Coke. She was fast asleep in Coke's arms while dancing in. Coke carefully took her to bed.

In the morning, when Ice woke up it was already very late. There was sunshine. Ice looked around and suddenly, she recalled something. She quickly came out of the camp. Coke and Khushi were playing with a ball while Saif was making tea.

"Why you people didn't wake me up? Even the clock in the camp…."

"Coke removed it since he wanted to see how long you can sleep if not disturbed."

Ice gave a glare at Coke.

"You know anger causes wrinkles at an early age. Now have a look at the surroundings and smile. I bet you must have never seen nature in such a wonderful form before."

Ice looked all around. She couldn't afford to blink her eyes to such beautiful scenery. Small and big hills surrounded the place; some were bearing green grass while others were covered with sand. Some peaks were covered with clouds. The sky was also like a colorful canvas. Two small springs emerging from the hills were presenting a breath taking view. The fresh breeze was a boon. There was a small ditch behind the camp. It looked as if diamonds were scattered. Coke showed all the views to Ice.

"I never thought that forests were so beautiful."

"All credit goes to grandpa for choosing such a wonderful place with unique atmosphere."

"Is there no fear of wild animals?"

"This you have to ask grandpa."

Saif came to them, "Who remembered me?"

"Grandpa, Ice is afraid of wild animals."

"I didn't say so."

"It's one or the same thing."

"How can it be the same thing? I was just…"

"Enough. Stop it. On seeing this ground, you shall notice a white line surrounding it. It is a magical friendship line. Any animal who happens to cross this line will assume you as its friend."

"You mean to say that there is no danger inside the ground."

"Exactly, outside it there are dangers. So, I will advise you to stay inside the limits."

"Grandpa, can we go to have a bath in the springs."

"Sure, be careful. Call me, if you see any danger."

Coke and Ice went to the spring. After a long time they were having some intimate moments. They were very happy. They enjoyed the cool water of spring.

After sometime Coke said, "Let's go Ice. Grandpa is calling us."

"No, let's stay for a while."

"Don't be a child. You are forgetting, we have not come here to have fun. You have to learn magic."

"Yes, I shall teach those goons…."

Suddenly, Ice remembered, "Oh! That man was supposed to take me today. Once he does not find me his face will be worth seeing."

Ice started running.

Coke ran after her, "Just a moment ago you didn't want to leave this place. Now what's the emergency?"

"I want to see the face of that goon."

"Is it so important?"

"Yes. The mannequins must have enjoyed it."

"Why don't you say that you are more concerned about mannequins instead of the goon?"

They reached the camp but grandpa was nowhere to be seen.

"Hey! Khushi, where is grandpa?"

"The mannequins have called him. He has left a message for you, not call him until it is necessary. Once the work is over he will be here. Your meal is ready. I had mine."

Khushi went away to play. Ice sat quietly in a corner.

"What happened? Aren't you feeling hungry?"

"No."

"I know Ice, you are missing the mannequins but just think whatever we are doing is to save them."

Coke cheered up Ice and after having their meals they waited for grandpa. Saif came before sunset. He was in a pleasant mood.

Ice was excited to see him, "What has happened over there?"

Coke said, "Seeing you I guess that something funny must have happened. Please tell us."

"Your guess is right, Coke. These mannequins are always busy doing one thing or the other."

"Grandpa, now tell us."

"The way mannequins made a fool of the goon is difficult to describe."

"Don't tell us, just show us what happened."

"That will be fine."

Saif showed his hand. Coke and Ice started watching. Khushi also joined them. The screen on Saif's hand was now showing Chunky entering the Mall. He made two rounds of the entire Mall but Ice was seen nowhere. He was angry with himself. At last he asked a girl working in the Mall. The girl was arranging Attu's clothes. She didn't listen to Chunky. Attu said in the girl's voice, "After two hours." Only the goon was able to hear this.

Chunky kept on waiting for two hours for Ice to come. Again he went to ask the girl. He was very furious. Now, he realized that he even didn't remember the face of that girl. Then he found another girl, "Can you tell me where is Ice?"

"Sir, tell me if I can help you?"

"No, I want to meet Ice only."

"Sorry Sir, she is off the duty today."

"Why?"

"You have to ask Mr. Robin regarding this."

The girl went away. Chunky was furious at the girl he asked earlier.

"I wish to shoot the girl who lied to me."

Dish said, "Attu, now he is planning to kill you."

Sitam said, "If he comes to know, he will knock you over."

Attu said, "I will show him who is going to be knocked over."

Chunky passed by Attu when he was talking over a phone. Attu quickly took his leg forward then pulled it back. Chunky had a nasty fall and collided with a glass vase. The vase was broken but Chunky suffered a severe head injury. Everybody ran to help him. He somehow managed to come out of the Mall and one of his associate seated him in the car. All the mannequins were very happy.

August said, "Hey! Attu, you did a wonderful job."

"I didn't do anything. One who digs a well for others is himself trapped in it."

Saif closed his hand. Coke was quiet while Ice was happy, "Attu did a great job."

Coke said, "But it was very risky job to do. If somebody had seen him, it could be a great trouble for him."

"Nobody did see."

"Grandpa, what about Chunky?"

"He is fine now but blames Ice for his sufferings. He will do anything to reach Ice."

"He will not succeed."

"Why not we tell him how to reach us?"

"Means?"

"I mean, let him see the jungle."

Ice was not getting the point but Coke's idea was very appealing to Saif. Ice learned some magic tricks from Saif. Instructing her to practice, Saif got busy with Coke to plan further. When Ice was through with her practice session and reached Saif's camp they were ready with their plan.

"You have made an excellent plan, Coke."

"Now we need younger grandpa's consent."

"You are worried about him but he will be more than happy once he listens the plan. He enjoys such things."

Then Coke saw Ice there, "When did you come? Is your practice over?"

"Yes, at least for today. Now, tell me about your plan."

"It will be great fun Ice. Coke, you tell her all the details meanwhile I visit Manas."

Before Ice could say anything, Saif disappeared. Coke told

Ice about the whole plan. Chunky and the boss were frustrated for not finding Ice.

"Our luck is not on our side. First she just escaped from my hand and then I got injured. Boss, once I find the girl, I will kill her."

"For that you have to find her first. Think, where can you find her."

"She has recently got married so nobody knows about her whereabouts."

Suddenly, Chunky's phone came to life.

"Hello. Is it Mr. Chunky?"

"Yes. Who's speaking?"

"I am Ice."

"From where did you get my number?"

"You gave it to Robin Sir. So I took it from him. Sorry, I couldn't do your work."

Chunky was now totally alert. He started to lay a trap for Ice. Ice pretended to be falling into his trap. It was decided that Chunky along with Manas will go to jungle to pick Ice then drop her back. Chunky was told that Manas knows the way to the camp. While Chunky was talking to Ice, Saif read his mind. If there has been any doubt in his mind Saif would have told Ice.

Chunky and his boss were making a different plan. They wanted to kill all of them in the jungle itself. All the specialized goons were ordered to get ready. In the morning when Manas saw so many people ready to go, he asked, "Who is Chunky among you?"

"It's me, Sir. These are my friends. We thought since we are going to jungle so why not enjoy some hunting."

"The rules don't allow killing deers or lions."

"We will go for birds only."

Manas was somewhat confused then he realized Saif's hand on his shoulder.

"You don't worry at all. You just send your car and driver back otherwise he will be killed."

Manas did what Saif said and after asking Chunky, he sent his car back. Chunky, boss and other goons mounted the jeep. Manas was guiding them to the camp which he didn't know. He gave further instructions following Saif. After roaming aimlessly for half an hour, Saif with his magic power blew a strong wind. The sand storm forced everybody to close their eyes and Saif took the jeep in the air and reached the camp site. Chunky stopped the jeep nervously.

"It's already half an hour. When are we going to reach?"

"We are about to make it. We just have to reach that ground in front of us."

Everybody was rubbing his eyes in an effort to clear them. Chunky started driving the jeep. Ice and Coke welcomed everybody. Goons were happy to see the surroundings.

Chunky asked, "Are you only two here?"

"No, no we are forty people here. All are nearby. Everyone will be here with a sound of single fire."

Coke lied knowingly. He also told Chunky before it gets dark most of the people will leave the place. After gathering all the information they decided to go on their hunting mission on the other side of the jungle across the ground.

"Boss, why did you refuse? We should have shot them there itself."

"Didn't you listen to the boy? One fire will attract everybody then what shall we do?"

Talking among themselves they proceeded further but Saif was with them. When they were thinking to return Saif produced a terrible lion's roar. They were not afraid; instead they were ready with their guns. When they were not able to spot the lion, they decided to track the animal. Saif guided them to the other side of the jungle.

On the other hand Manas, Coke and Ice were resting for a while after having meals. Saif had to be back according to plan.

"I will ask grandpa, where is he?"

"Can't you wait for a little?"

"There is no harm in asking."

"We know everything, then why do we ask?"

Manas who was listening their arguments commented, "It looks you two have transformed to be real husband and wife."

Embarrassment made them quiet.

"Hey! Why did you go into silent mode? Please continue. Otherwise in my profession, I get seldom chances to hear arguments though I argue a lot."

"Grandpa the junior, you are pulling my leg. I will not speak to you."

Ice left the place.

"What's wrong with her?"

"Leave it grandpa. Girls are like this only. You are lucky as you are still single."

"Don't try to be smart. After a while you will be after her to make up with her."

Coke smiled. Then they heard Saif's voice.

"What's going on here?"

Ice came running, "Grandpa, you don't listen to them. First tell me whether everything was alright."

"Exactly, all went according to plan but the technique was different."

"We can't get it."

"They were not frightened by lion's roar but tried to find and kill it."

"That's why it took you so long to distract them from their way."

"All is well that ends well."

Seeing Coke quiet, Saif asked, "Hey! Coke, why are you so quiet?"

"I was thinking whether it was right on our part to leave such brave people in the jungle to die. They must be having families. What will happen to them?"

"It was you who made the plan. Then you should also think, we are not killing anybody."

"I admit, it was my plan but we will be the reason for their death and while making the plan I never considered their families."

"Coke is right grandpa. We should let them go."

"If we leave them they will not leave us alive."

Manas said, "There must be some way out. We shall find a way in which no life is lost and they learn the lesson too."

Saif immediately left for the safety of those people. Manas, Coke and Ice went to their camps to sleep. Though all were not sleepy at all and they were thinking for an easy way out. At morning tea, all were waiting for Saif. Saif told them that he was late because he went to see the mannequins.

Manas asked, "Saif, how is the boss and his goons?"

"Not that good. I guarded them the whole night. They are hungry and thirsty. Still they have not lost courage. They are confident; today they will find their way to the city."

"We have to wait until their confidence is shattered."

"After that?"

"The people who part death to others should themselves experience the turmoil."

"What do you think Manas?"

"You know how to read minds, so get ahead."

"It is very fearful to enter the minds of advocates. There always have some arguments going on."

"Nothing like this. People have given us bad name for nothing. When there is no need we don't indulge in arguments."

"Like…."

"Since you are short of brains with you, did I ever start an argument with you?"

"Both of you are in a funny mood but let's make the further plan."

"The next program is that you learn magic from Saif and I and Coke will have a game of chess."

"Nice idea. I will get one right now."

Ice knew that Manas needed time to work out over the whole plan. She left with Saif. So this day also passed. The night had taken in the jungle and the goons were loosing hopes.

"I think we shall never be able to find our way out from this jungle."

"We never thought that we shall loose our lives just for an ordinary girl."

Boss shouted, "Who says that we shall loose lives? Have some courage."

"Don't give false hopes. I am dying due to thirst. It is better to shoot myself instead of such a death."

"He is right. We are only left with the bullets to eat."

There conversation continued. They were lying lifeless. They were alive but their courage was fading away fast. In the end, four of them decided to shoot themselves. Saif was seeing and listening everything. They took out their guns. Saif was not sure of what to do. Suddenly, he spoke, "Just stop."

They were startled and looked all around.

"Who are you? Talk to us face to face."

"I am right in front of you."

"Where?"

"The tree under which you are sitting, I am the ghost of that tree."

"We don't believe in ghosts."

"As you wish. I just wanted to help you out."

Chunky said in a sad tone, "Can you manage to take us out of this jungle?"

"Yes, I can."

The second one said, "He is making fool of us."

"What would I get by making a fool out of you?"

"You want to kill us."

"Even if I do not kill you, within two or three days you are going to die. You were just planning to kill yourself right now."

"He is right. We have to die, so why do we not listen him?"

"Will you show us the way?"

"Sure, but you have to make a promise that you will leave this evil path forever."

"You mean to say that we go to police and spend rest of our lives in the prison."

"Then, what's the fun of getting out of here?"

Saif said, "I didn't mean that. You forget whatever has happened and spend a life of ordinary people by doing hard work."

They were looking at each other. Saif was reading there minds. It was not easy to get rid of life which they were so used to.

The boss said, "How can we accept that you will take us out off this jungle as we are unable to walk even."

"You stay here, I will be back shortly."

Within no time Saif reached the camps. He narrated the whole story. After much thought they reached the conclusion that it will not be safe to take them out of the jungle so early. They were hungry as well as thirsty. It was important to keep them alive too so that they adopt the right path in life. Saif took some eatables in the jeep and went back. Seeing jeep without a driver they were shocked. Jeep halted in front of them.

"Who drove it here?"

"It was me so that you can have faith in what I tell you. There are a few things to eat so you eat first."

All of them felt a new energy in their bodies. Saif was thinking what he will talk to them after they finish eating but in the meantime he heard August calling him from the Mall.

"Saif, where are you. Come immediately."

Saif reached the Mall, "What's the matter?"

Saif noticed mannequins were busy in some discussion. They all surrounded Saif.

"Saif, the people who want to sell the Mall were here today. They were asking for some information about Ice."

They were looking quite upset as they knew about their people are lost in the jungle."

"Chunky must have informed them over his mobile."

"Now what will happen, Saif?"

"There is no need to worry. We shall go to the court directly."

"Since they were talking, we think they shall not let Ice reach the court at any cost."

"Perhaps, they are aware that they will not be able to stand before Manas with their fake documents in court."

"That's for sure."

"I think something must be done for these people like those goons."

"What happened to them? Are they dead?"

Saif provided them with all details and again they started their discussions. In the morning, Saif was back in the jungle. When he saw whole of the gang sleeping, he returned to the camp. Saif saw Manas lost in his thoughts.

"Here you are sitting like an owl. Why do you show like this when you are already one?"

Manas was not surprised, "I am in no mood of joking."

"I am also serious."

Manas didn't reply. He covered his face and went to sleep.

Saif smiled over this and said, "You have become so old but your habits are still like that of a child. I know this behaviour right from your childhood. When things don't go your way, you behave like this."

Saif pulled the sheet which Manas pulled back. Saif decided to have some fun and by his magic spell he made the sheet tied all around his body. Now Manas was unable to cover his face.

He shouted, "Hey! Don't try your magic on me. Otherwise......"

"What will you do? You will file a case against me or shoot me?" Saif laughed and untied the sheet.

"Your body is dead, now I doubt that your heart is dead as well."

"Why don't you say straightaway?"

"The matter is not so simple. You know that Ice and Coke are in a great danger?"

Coke and Ice also heard them shouting.

"What is going on in grandpa's camp, I will go and check it out."

"Nothing serious. They are fighting on some issue. You sleep."

"How do you know?"

Ice gave him a hard stare.

"O.K., I got it."

They went to sleep. Saif was trying to convince Manas, "What's wrong with you Manas. For so many years you were not afraid of anything. Even the dangerous culprits are afraid of you."

"I was not afraid because I had no weakness."

"So what has gone wrong now?"

"I am in love."

"At this age?"

"Saif, I am in no mood to joke."

"You know how bad your face becomes when you are angry?"

Manas again pulled the sheet and went to sleep. Saif was smiling. Thus he said, "O.K., no more jokes now. I know, you love Coke and Ice very much. Nothing will happen to them. I am always with them."

It took quite a time to Saif to calm down Manas. It was dawn. Saif went to the gang. Some of them were sleeping while others were awake. Saif started listening their talks.

"Boss, what do you think? Should we believe in the so called ghost?"

"I don't believe in ghosts. There is nothing like it. This is just a name to make people afraid."

"O.K., I agree, what you say is perfectly true, but you also heard the sound."

"Leave it. From where did the jeep come?"

"I thought we will find our way in the jeep but we can't

even drive it in this dense forest. But how did he managed to bring it here?"

'I think he is a magician, who…."

Boss shouted, "Shut up all of you, otherwise I will shoot your brains out."

Chunky said, "Boss it's of no use to shout like this. You are unmarried and have no parents. But all of us have families. How will they live without us? I have to go."

"O.K., whoever wants to leave can go. I will not accept defeat."

Finding the right opportunity Saif made his presence felt. Saif let them take the oath of their family members and in the blink of an eye they were on the road leading to the city. They were in the jeep. The boss was now all alone in the jungle. All of them thanked Saif, once they were out of the jungle. They left their guns in the jeep and started towards their homes. Saif hid the jeep in the jungle.

Coke and Ice were very happy in the jungle. From time to time Saif gave Ice magic lessons. Manas went back to the city. With the help of the mannequins Saif knew the whereabouts of Sikander. Sikander's son was Kasim. Saif came to know that it was Sikander who killed Ice's parents. One day, Saif reached the marvelous Bungalow of Sikander. He noticed Sikander was very upset. He was having a walk in his room. Perhaps he was waiting for somebody to come. The very moment Kasim came out of the car. He came upstairs at a brisk speed.

"Have you got any information?"

"No, Dad. Nothing."

"Only two days are left for the hearing to start and….."

"It is all your fault Dad. I had already told you to get rid of the girl. You were against killing her."

"I thought it to be an easy job, now I have no idea where the girl is and the Boss is also missing. They had just disappeared."

"You listen to me. We should kill the advocate. Once he is finished there is no other advocate to whom we cannot buy."

"That is fine. I don't want to take any risk."

"There is no risk involved, Dad. The person who kills the advocate will have to leave this city forever. Nobody will doubt us. Moreover Manas also has many enemies."

"Fine. Do whatever you think is right."

Kasim gave some instructions over the phone. Saif reached Manas and told him the whole story.

"They want to finish me off."

"Yes, you don't leave house tomorrow."

"Now, who is talking like a coward?"

"Please try to understand Manas. I don't know how they are going to attack you. Once I get the information, we shall find the way out."

"It is very important for us to reach the court tomorrow. We have to think of something else."

"O.K., you shall not use your regular car tomorrow. You shall go by some other means."

"I can do so."

The next day Manas's car left the Bungalow at the right time. Saif was on the roof of the car. After a while, a white car was following them. Saif went into that car. A fat bald person was driving the car. There was nobody else in the car. He was trying to contact someone on the mobile.

"Sir, his car is ahead of us. I shall shoot him at some signal. It will be easy to flee away from the scene."

Saif couldn't hear what was said at the other end, the phone was disconnected. After some distance, the bald person stopped Manas's car. He went to him.

"What's the matter, Sir? Why did you stop my car?"

"I am from CID. I need to search your car."

"You are mistaken, Sir. This car belongs to an advocate."

"O.K., then I can speak to the advocate. I can clear my doubts on talking to him."

"O.K. Sir, I will call him over the phone."

The fat man was surprised, "Why? Is he not in the car?"

"No, Sir has gone somewhere else."

"Why are you driving the car alone?"

"Big people have their own styles. I am just a servant."

The fat man was now very furious. He was confused thinking what to do. Suddenly, he took his wallet out to bribe the driver with several hundred rupee notes. He gave it to the driver who was very happy to take them.

"What do you want, Sir?"

"Wherever your Sir goes today keep me informed."

"It won't create trouble to me?"

"No, I just want to meet him once."

The bulky fellow gave the driver his number. When the fellow was gone the driver informed Manas about occurring.

"Sir, the person was not good. Your life is in danger."

"Don't worry Gopal, tell him on the phone that I am going the Mall and shall be there till evening."

"Right Sir."

Saif was confused hearing Manas. He went to Manas, "Why did you call him of your being in the Mall?"

"I have listened many deeds of your mannequins, so I thought to test them. Are they worth it or not?"

"Your life is in danger and you are planning to slaughter others! By the way who told you about the mannequins?"

"You know Saif the wisdom of long fellows is in their knees. The short persons like me have their brains at the right place."

"This discovery is done by you or by some dwarf scientist?"

"I shall tell you later. Right now, I am going to the court. You also go to the Mall to welcome that bulky fellow."

"We shall welcome him in such a manner which he will remember for his whole life."

Saif reached the Mall and discussed the matter with the mannequins.

August said, "That fatty person wants to kill Manas. How?"

Sitam said, "If we come to know his plan then we can make out a counter plan."

Jenny said, "Dish, first of all you keep an eye on every fat person who comes here. Saif, you just point him to us then we shall manage him."

Ferry said, "It is good, today is not a working day and the Mall has no customers."

Jui said, "It will be a great fun."

Saif said, "This sounds good, you all should be careful."

Dish thus sent a message, "Saif, a person of your description is here."

Saif looked around and immediately recognized the person.

That person started having a walk in the Mall. Everybody was reading his mind.

"As soon as the advocate turns up, I shall shoot him and flee away. Oh, I just forgot to get my pistol from my shoe."

He dashed to the bathroom. Saif was behind him. He opened his zipped shoe and took out a small pistol which he secured it in his jacket.

Saif was thinking, "So this is how he came inside unnoticed of pistol by the guards. The criminal can go to any extent."

The fatty's eyes were glued at the main gate. Manas informed Saif of his arrival. Saif saw the man ready with his hand on his gun. Saif thought, he would shoot Manas as soon as he enters the Mall. He sent a message to Manas, "You wait outside, enter the Mall when I signal you."

As long as the fat man was scanning the main eneterance it was not possible for Manas to come inside. All the mannequins were lost deep in thoughts. The fat man passed in front of Attu. Attu had a chain in his hand. He struck its hook in his jacket. He stopped while walking. He tried to loose the hook from his jacket which gave a fair chance for Manas to enter the Mall. The fat man was angry. He growled at Attu.

"Have you been alive, I would have shot you?"

Attu replied, "You are threatening me. See, what we do with you today."

Though the fat man could not hear him. He followed Manas at a brisk pace. All the mannequins and Saif were hiding Manas from him. Whenever the fat fellow comes down Manas was seen upstairs. Whatever the fat man thought, mannequins received the message and transmitted it to Saif who in turn instructed Manas. When he took stairs, Manas was on the ground floor and vanished with in a blink of an eye. An hour passed in this exercise. The fat man was very tired but Manas and the mannequins were having fun.

Then Saif asked Manas to reach trial room, "You stay there, I shall be there shortly."

Saif saw, the fat man has noticed Manas and he stood in front of the door. His hands were in his pocket and he was alert and ready.

Saif came back to Manas, "Close your eyes."

"Why?"

"No questions. Be quick."

Manas closed his eyes and immediately Saif asked him, "You can open your eyes now."

"Hey! where are we?"

"You are in your car. Go to your home."

"Why did you take me outside? I was having fun. It was just like a game we played in childhood."

"You have no idea if you had been out of this trial room that person would have shot you."

"What is going to happen now?"

"He is waiting for you over there; I shall fail the brakes of his car. You go home."

"It's a good plan."

Manas called his driver, "Gopal, let's go home."

"Sir, how did you enter the car? It was locked."

"It might be unlocked by mistake. Now don't talk, we have to leave this place quickly."

Gopal raced the car and Manas was gone. In the Mall, the fat man was standing outside the trial room for half an hour and was furious by now. Saif also came back after completing his work.

Dish asked, "Saif if he had fired at Manas, he also would have caught?"

"His pistol has got a silencer to suppress the sound of fire. By the time people would know of the happenings, he would have gone from the scene."

Jui said, "Whatever you say Saif, it was great fun."

"The real fun is still to come. The fat man is now moving in."

Attu shouted, "I can't see anything. Tell me what's happening."

"Be patient. I will show you in the night."

"No, I want it now."

"It is not possible."

"You can give me a running commentary."

"O.K. Here you go."

Saif started narrating, "The fat man is going towards trial room at a slow pace with anger on his face. His brain is totally confused. One of his hands is in his pocket and he carefully opened the door. The door opened quite easily against his expectations but the trial room is empty. He cannot believe his eyes. He is searching the small trial room with his eyes wide opened."

All the mannequins were enjoying Saif's commentary. Now Saif was talking at a brisk pace. "The fatty is out of the room being very much confused. He checked the entire the Mall but in vain. Now pulling his hair he is heading towards washroom. He put the pistol back into its place and relieved himself. Now he is coming out of the Mall with heavy steps."

All the mannequins were laughing and Saif took his seat in fat man's car. The fat man was wondering, "Where that dwarf had eloped? I never left the place. If somebody else had said the same thing to me, I should've never believed. What shall I tell Kasim. He will not believe me either."

He was driving lost it in his thoughts, suddenly; he realized the brakes are not working. In an effort to save himself he collided the car with a wall. He got serious injuries but was alive.

Saif had a close look at him, "Now, there is no danger from him. The case will be decided till he gets well."

Saif went to jungle and detailed the further program, "Get ready kids, tomorrow we have to reach the court."

"Younger grandpa is fine?"

"He is perfectly fine. Rest of the things will be discussed later on."

Saif then went to Sikander's house. Here, what he saw was astonishing. Sikander was shouting at his son.

"You were very confident. What happened now? I feel we shall lose everything."

"I shall not accept defeat so easily."

"Nothing can be done now. Tomorrow, we have to answer the questions of the advocate."

Disappointed Sikander went to sleep but Kasim was thinking of a fresh plan.

Saif thought, "He is young blood, so I have to keep an eye on him."

Next morning court was very crowded. Media has got the news. Sikander was a known personality of the town. People were not aware of his evil aspect. As soon as Ice descended the car she was surrounded by media personnel.

"You are fighting with such a big name?"

"If you are the real owner then why were you silent for so long?"

"Is it the working in the Mall which gave you the feeling that you own it?"

So many questions were there. Ice was calm with Coke by her side. She never responded to any of the questions. Manas came and took them inside. The proceedings started once the judge had arrived. Sikander and Ice were looking at each other for the first time. While Ice was looking at him with hatred, Kasim was watching Ice with furious looks.

Manas was skilled at his work. His counter questions were difficult to be handled for the opposition lawyer. Court asked for some more documents from Sikander, then his lawyer asked for some extra time. Manas played his part cleverly. He took the plea that Ice's life was at risk for which the next hearing was fixed after two days.

While returning home Kasim blocked Ice's way, "You have to pay for it. It's because of you that my dad is so worried and tense."

"Is it? Then I should be angrier than you as your Dad has murdered my parents."

Kasim was taken aback as he was not expecting this from Ice. He was shocked, how could Ice knew it?

"How could I know this? This is what you are thinking?"

"No, this is not true. You have no proof."

"You are right. If I had proof then I wouldn't have been silent. Now both of us know the reality."

Ice went to her car. When Sikander came to know about all this from Kasim, he lost his senses.

"This means that after winning this case, she is going to sue me for murder."

"She cannot do this Dad. She has no proof."

"She has not today but after winning the case, the people will come to know about her strength and truthfulness. This question will also emerge, where did the real owners of the Mall had disappeared. Every answer will give birth to a new question. All the fingers will be pointing at me. My political carrier will also end. All the respect I earned will be finished. I can see myself behind the bars right now."

"Calm down, Dad. You are accepting defeat even before defeat."

"I can see no hope."

Then came their lawyer, "There is still a way out."

"What's it?"

"We have to tell the court that all the documents are destroyed in fire."

"How?"

"I have an idea. My office is in the Mall. Let's blow up the Mall."

"This is too risky."

"The damage will be of crores of rupees."

"Respect will be saved. The loss is inevitable even if we lose the case."

"Kasim is right."

"O.K., you do whatever you feel is right. I will take your leave. But keep in mind that we have only one day left."

The advocate left the place and father and son started working on a fresh strategy. Sikander didn't want to faith anybody. He decided to do the job himself.

"Dad, give it one more thought."

"You don't worry. I used to work in a mine. I know this very well. Tomorrow we shall be ready with all the materials and execute our plan at night."

Saif reached Manas' house. Coke and Ice were also there due to security reasons. They were having their meals. Khushi barked.

Ice said, "Grandpa has come."

Manas said, "We are enjoying our food please don't spoil it with some bad news. It is better not to see your face otherwise you would've spoiled it."

The servant serving the dinner became nervous, "Sir, whom you are talking to? Nobody is here."

Manas was surprised, "Is it so! Ice, you just uttered something."

Ice handled the situation, "I was just joking."

"Don't make such jokes, people here will think me as crazy."

The servant were more confused, "Sorry, Sir, I didn't mean that."

"You can go now. We shall call you if needed."

"Yes, Sir."

He went off. After he was gone, Coke had a hearty laugh which he was suppressing with great difficulty.

"Hey! Younger grandpa, you were just to create a trouble."

"This dwarf has no sense."

"Why? Haven't you seen him in the court getting to the nerves of their advocate?"

"He is so happy as if he has already won the case."

"Take it as won. Today I got all their pleas rejected. They are left with nothing."

"Yes, they too know this and that is why they have turned so dangerous."

Coke said, "Grandpa, what is their fresh plan?"

"They are going to blow up the Mall."

Three of them were stunned, "What?"

"Have they gone crazy?"

"What shall they get from doing this?"

"They don't care for it but they don't want to see you getting rights. This is not in their nature."

"What shall we do now?"

"I and the mannequins will take care of the Mall."

"We shall be around the Mall."

"No, Ice, people will doubt us for which we have to face them."

"How?"

"Tomorrow I will arrange a party at my house and invite some big shots of the city."

"A party for what?"

"Big people celebrate their birthday four times in a year; he will also do the same."

"Don't make fun of me Saif but idea is not bad at all."

Everything was decided and they left to sleep. Nobody was able to sleep. Sikander was having a restless night while Kasim was calming down his nerves with alcohol. Manas was preparing a list of the invitees. Ice was trying her best to sleep while Coke was watching her.

"Why are you staring at me like an owl?"

"So I cannot see you even. Tomorrow you shall ask why I am in your room."

"Coke don't change the topic. You know what I am doing. I am not getting any sleep."

"That is what I am saying. Why are you trying to sleep then?"

"What else should I do?"

"You can read a book as I do or watch television. Try to distract your thoughts. This will help you to get some sleep."

"I am quite worried about the mannequins."

"You are worrying without any reason. The magic of grandpa is great and mannequins are with him too. I was thinking of those father and son what will happen to them. They are going to get a lesson on the hands of those lifeless mannequins."

Ice smiled and closed her eyes. At the Mall, Saif was organizing his army. They all were very happy to listen him.

Jenny said, "I am already feeling happy for we are also going to be a part of this war."

Amber said, "Saif, we shall teach such a good lesson to these murderers in which they shall not be able to identify their face."

Jui said, "They are going to see tomorrow, I bet they have not seen it in their entire lives."

Sitam said, "I just want to see the expression on the faces of killers when they themselves face death."

August said, "Now Saif, first of all you tell us your plan."

Saif said, "They will lay wires in the Mall. I am not sure that they want to blow up the entire Mall or just a portion of it."

Ferry said, "Wherever they shall lay the wires we shall cut them."

"This is very easy but I don't want to do this."

"What is your plan Saif?"

"I want the bomb should blow in which father and son duo blew apart in the explosion. Court will take its own time but I want to punish them myself."

"Whatever you say, we shall do."

"First we will have to locate the portion of the Mall where the explosion does not have any effect on you. I have got a map of Mall with me."

Then they started making their plan. After much survey, they could not find a place from where the explosion will not harm them. At last, they got success. Next day Sikander and Kasim collected the material required. Ice stopped Manas from going to the Mall. She and Coke were busy making arrangements for the party. Sikander reached the Mall in the evening. Kasim followed after sometime. They put all the material in their office.

"Sir, it is time to close the Mall."

"We have a lot of work to do so we will stay late in the night."

"Sir, it is against rules."

Kasim came to him and offered him some money. He looked at them.

"Now you can leave but be sure not to start alarm until we are here."

"Right, Sir."

He went away and they got busy with their work. After sometime the lights of the Mall went off. Their office was on upper floor. They started to lay the wires from the top. It was pitch dark and they were using a small torch. But mannequins had no such problem, they were already active. When Sikander and Kasim were laying wires in the staircase Saif was replacing them with duplicate ones. For Saif it was an easy magic trick.

Sikander was planting a bomb just besides Attu. His back was towards Attu. Attu bending a little and extended his hands towards his neck. He would have choked him if Ferry had not interfered.

"Are you mad?"

"It is him who is crazy. I am doing what I should do."

"I know but this is not the right way. It is not in our plan."

"I cannot control myself."

Suddenly, Sikander turned around and Attu and Ferry had no time to recover. They were standing still holding each others hands. Sikander pointed the torch at them, "When I came here only one mannequin was present but I can see two now."

He thought, "Perhaps I paid no attention at that time. It is so dark. I should finish my work."

Leaving his thoughts aside he got busy with his work.

Ferry said, "Stand still Attu until he leaves the place."

"It is not sure for he will go by himself."

"If you will do anything wrong I will tell Saif…."

Ferry didn't got the chance to say anything as Attu threw a great kick on Sikander's back. He was caught totally unaware. He jumped in the air and collided with a rack. Then rack was over him. Jenny, John and Jui also joined Attu and Ferry. There was no movement for sometime.

John said, "I think he is dead."

Ferry shouted, "You should have controlled yourself Attu."

"How could I? You know he was telling bad names to Ice and her family. Reading minds of such people is just like finding some lost thing in a dustbin."

Then came out Sikander's hand out of the clothes piled on the rack. He was struggling to come out. On the other hand Kasim was going to face something more serious. He put the bomb in the pocket of Sitam and started looking at him. Both of his hands were busy working while he was holding the torch with his mouth.

"I would have enjoyed more if you were alive. The fact is in fighting we enjoy when the enemy is equal in stature.

Sitam took the bomb and placed it in Kasim's pocket. Sitam was aware that Kasim could not hear him so he gestured with his hand to make him understand. Kasim didn't get him.

"I think you want to say me something but I can't understand dumb mannequin."

Kasim turned for a while then suddenly it strike to him, to whom he was talking to. He couldn't believe it and went back to Sitam. Sitam was now standing like a mannequin.

"How can you talk to me? Mannequins never speak. It is my illusion. You put the bomb in my pocket and...."

Kasim stopped in between and put his hand in his pocket to find the bomb. He became nervous.

"You....... me......... talk..., made a .....gesture....... you.......can......only........move."

The mannequin still didn't move. Kasim dared to touch it.

"Dad is right. Too much of alcohol affects your senses. I

should not indulge myself in these silly things. Let's get on with the job."

Kasim held the torch with his mouth and again started to put the bomb in Sitam's pocket. Sitam gave a powerful slap on his face. Kasim was on the floor while torch was in the air. August caught it. Amber, Dish and Jui also came. August switched off the torch. Kasim was not able to see anything but he had a feeling as if he was surrounded by some people.

"Who are you? What do you want? I will kill you all."

Kasim took a gun out of his pocket and fired at mannequins. August could have got hurt if Saif hadn't intervened. Kasim didn't get the second chance. Saif got hold of his gun and mannequins were all over him. He was shouting leave me, leave me.

Dish said, "What should we do with him, Saif?"

"First of all make him stop shouting."

Sitam got a scarf with which they tied his mouth.

"Let's take him to Sikander."

All of them gathered at the centre of the Mall. Saif made place for them. Once the rack was removed Sikander stood up. He had a light wound on his forehead and a little blood was also there. He was looking for his torch. Mannequins took Kasim to him. He touched Kasim.

"Hey! Kasim, why did you kick me?"

"Kasim was not able to speak. Mannequins freed his arms. He got hold of Sikander's hand and started swaying it like a crazy person. He was not able to remove the scarf from his mouth as Saif had tied it with his magic spell. Sikander was horrified at Kasim's crazy behaviour. The mannequins and Saif were having fun at father and the son duo.

"Why don't you speak? Speak with your mouth."

Kasim touched Sikander's hand on his face.

"Why have you tied your mouth? Open it."

Sikander tried to help but nothing happened. Dish gave both the torches in Kasim's hands and stood like a mannequin. Kasim lit both the torches. Now father and son can look at each other. Now Kasim tried with the gestures of his hand so that his father could understand. Though his way was a bit awkward but father was even greater. He interpreted all the meanings wrong. Kasim pointed towards the mannequins and then walked like them to show his father.

"Kasim, you have gone mad. Why should I make these mannequins walk? We are here for something different."

Kasim again made some gestures. Sikander looked at all the mannequins surrounding them.

"You, idiot, why did you bring all these mannequins here? I told you to bring the bomb."

One of the mannequins quietly placed the bomb in Sikander's pocket. Kasim noticed this and showed the bomb to Sikander. Sikander slapped him and said, "You planted the bomb in my pocket. You want to explode me?"

The mannequins were moving in front of Kasim but for Sikander they were mannequins. Kasim couldn't make Sikander understand. Tired, he sat aside. Mannequins were having a good laugh. After sometime Saif said, "I think we have had enough fun. Manas has also sent me message. We have to get over with this within half an hour before the party starts over there."

As per the plan, mannequins took Sikander and Kasim on the top floor where Sikander's office was situated. They tied many bombs around Kasim. After that they arranged a dim light so that Sikander can have a look. Seeing his son's condition Sikander got crazy. He wanted to go ahead but mannequins were holding him back. He could not believe this. Fear and horror didn't let him speak.

"So this was…. what you…… w…anted to tell me?"

Kasim nodded. Mannequins took Kasim near the window and gave the remote in Sikander's hands. Attu gestured at him to press the button.

"No, I can't do this. My son will explode."

Mannequins gave him many slaps. Dish took out his pistol and fixed it on his head.

"I shall die myself but not kill my son."

Dish asked, "Saif should I go ahead?"

"No, we will not kill him. He will die himself while watching his son explode. All of you go to a safe place before the explosion takes place."

"These two…."

"My magic will take care of them both."

Saif threw his magic spell and both of them became mannequins.

"Now they shall dance to my tunes."

All the mannequins went to their places. Saif rearranged the Mall. Then he came to Sikander's office. He put the remote in Sikander's hand and placed his finger on the button. He opened the window and threw Kasim out of it. While Kasim was going down he made Sikander to push his finger on the button. The bombs exploded along with Kasim. Sikander shouted loudly but no one was there to listen him. He got unconscious.

With Saif's clever plan building was unharmed. Hearing explosion security guards came.

Saif went to mannequins, "All is well, now I am going to Manas."

Ferry said, "But Sikander is still alive and he knows our reality."

"I know but people shall think him as a mad person because of his son's grief."

The lights of the Mall came to effect and Saif went to Ice.

The guests at the party were about to leave. They were watching Ice and Coke dance. When Ice felt Saif's presence, she stopped dancing.

"What happened Ice?"

"Coke, I am tired."

All the guests clapped. Ice informed Coke and Manas about Saif's arrival. At that very moment the mobile of a senior police office rang.

"Hello……..O.K……..when…….I am coming."

Manas said, "I think you have to go. Perhaps something important has come up."

"You are right and it is more important to you than me."

"Tell me, what is it?"

"The Mall for which you are fighting the case has been tried to be blow up."

"Who is going to get any benefit by doing so?"

Ice came forward, "Has Mall suffered any harm?"

"Still no such information, I have to reach the place first."

After the guests were gone, Saif told the whole story. For the next few days Ice and Manas made the news headlines. The case was won without any problem. The Mall and its land was now transferred in Ice's name.

Sikander was caught with a bomb. He was declared a culprit but due to his crazy talks court sent him to a mental asylum.

Ice was now the new owner of the Mall. When she reached the Mall everybody welcomed her. Mr. Robin guided her to office.

"Sit here Madam. This chair belongs to you now."

"This is your chair, Sir and it will remain only yours and don't call me madam."

"If I sit here then what shall you do?"

"I and Coke has decided to launch a brand."

Ice now could not have managed to be with the mannequins for entire day. So they got there house constructed on the top floor of the Mall. Now they had a big family. At night they came down and had great fun with mannequins. Khushi had also grown up.

Whenever mannequins had something new they called Ice. Today great dance and fun was going in the Mall. It was the first time that Ice was watching mannequins dance.

"You people can dance too?"

Coke was laughing but not in front of Ice as he knew if Ice see him laughing at the mannequins, she will be angry with him. He didn't want to do so as it was their first wedding anniversary and moreover he was about to become a father.

Are you interested in writing Romantic Novels? Do you want them to be published? Here is an opportunity for you. Contact: nk@dbp.in

www.ingramcontent.com/pod-product-compliance
Lightning Source LLC
Chambersburg PA
CBHW071214260626
47162CB00004B/1286